PUFFIN B

SMUGGLERS

'It's dangerous,' said Reuben quietly.
'Transportation to the colonies if we're
caught. Or hanging.'
'Doesn't frighten me, I've been close to
both before now,' said Pin.

Christopher Russell was a postman when he had his first radio play broadcast in 1975, having given up a job in the Civil Service to do shift work and have more daytime hours for writing. Since 1980, he has been a full-time scriptwriter and has worked on numerous television and radio programmes. Christopher lives with his wife on the Isle of Wight.

Books by Christopher Russell

BRIND AND THE DOGS OF WAR

PLAGUE SORCERER

SMUGGLERS!

SMUGGLERS

CHRISTOPHER RUSSELL

PUFFIN

PUFFIN BOOKS

Published by the Penguin Group
Penguin Books Ltd, 80 Strand, London WC2R ORL, England
Penguin Group (USA) Inc., 375 Hudson Street, New York, New York 10014, USA
Penguin Group (Canada), 90 Eglinton Avenue East, Suite 700, Toronto, Ontario, Canada M4P 2Y3
(a division of Pearson Penguin Canada Inc.)
Penguin Ireland, 25 St Stephen's Green, Dublin 2, Ireland (a division of Penguin Books Ltd)
Penguin Group (Australia), 250 Camberwell Road, Camberwell, Victoria 3124, Australia
(a division of Pearson Australia Group Pty Ltd)
Penguin Books India Pvt Ltd, 11 Community Centre, Panchsheel Park, New Delhi – 110 017, India
Penguin Group (NZ), 67 Apollo Drive, Mairangi Bay, Auckland 1310, New Zealand
(a division of Pearson New Zealand Ltd)
Penguin Books (South Africa) (Pty) Ltd, 24 Sturdee Avenue, Rosebank, Johannesburg 2196, South Africa

Penguin Books Ltd, Registered Offices: 80 Strand, London WC2R ORL, England

penguin.com

Published 2007
2

Text copyright © Christopher Russell, 2007
All rights reserved

The moral right of the author has been asserted

Set in Monotype Baskerville by Palimpsest Book Production Limited, Grangemouth, Stirlingshire
Made and printed in England by Clays Ltd, St Ives plc

British Library Cataloguing in Publication Data
A CIP catalogue record for this book is available from the British Library

ISBN: 978-0-141-32095-3

This book is dedicated to Diana,
a big person in a small package

Contents

1. From the Sea   1

2. Blue-Coats   14

3. The Broken Net   33

4. Black Tooth   54

5. Treason   74

6. Interrogation   98

7. Chantry Cove   117

8. Burial   129

9. The Rifle   148

10. House Wreck   164

11. Asher   173

12. Justice   184

I

From the Sea

It was a long way down. The stones dislodged by Reuben's feet took several seconds to bounce into the sea far below. The sea swallowed them but wanted more – it wanted Reuben Hibberd. It threw itself at the crumbling, chalky cliff, roaring and stretching long fingers of hissing foam up towards him. The spray drenched Reuben's back and made the tarred rope from which he dangled slippery. He clung on, shutting out his dread of the sea and swinging himself towards the next ledge.

The stench of a thousand nesting seabirds made Reuben gasp and their screeching din battered his ears but when the mother razorbill scuttled forward with raised wings and gaping beak, he swung his stick unerringly. He killed the bird with a single blow and stuffed it in his bag, then grabbed the helpless grey-white chick and thrust that in as well. The bag was full now. Reuben would get his eightpence for the feathers and sixpence for the dozen or so carcases. A shilling and twopence altogether. His family could afford to eat.

Reuben hauled himself back to the clifftop. He was always relieved to feel the turf beneath his feet again. Relieved that the iron spike to which he tied his rope had once again held firm, supported his weight. He was only twelve years old but growing fast. Still agile but getting too big and heavy to be a cliff boy. If ever the spike or the rope or the cliff edge gave way, he would be dead.

Reuben coiled the rope and headed for home. It had been a fine morning when he'd set out for the Cormorant Cliff. He'd dared to hope that summer was finally arriving. But the wind had freshened and now he could see another storm piling up on the horizon. Yet more rain coming, after a cold wet winter and an even wetter spring. Heavy rain was his family's biggest enemy: it led to rock falls and landslides. Dangerous enough up here on the high chalk cliff but more menacing still down in the bay, where he and the other beach-dwellers lived in their fragile cottages perched above the tideline. The cliff down there behind the cottages was low but it was even less sturdy than the high chalk. It was formed instead of layers of sand and mudstone through which streams oozed and trickled to the shore. In places, after prolonged rain had swollen the streams, it looked more like a sloping bog than a wall of rock.

A track led to the shore from the nearby village but the most recent landslide had carried the end of the track into the sea. Reuben climbed down the rickety wooden ladder that had been built to replace it, and stood on the beach for a moment. Eventually, the two cottages, like the track above, would be swallowed by the sliding grey mud and Reuben and his family would have no choice but to move. But not this year, Reuben told himself. A warm dry summer would assure them of that. He tried to ignore the first spatter of rain on the wind.

A tall gangling figure was hobbling to meet him. Reuben's grandfather. He was hobbling because he had only one foot. The other had been smashed by a cannonball in a sea battle when he'd been a sailor.

'Best get them birds plucked sharpish,' he said. 'You could be busy later.'

Reuben saw that his grandfather had his telescope with him. He was off to the cliffs to watch for ships. Ships in trouble in the brewing storm. Reuben himself was keen to get indoors for some breakfast.

The Hibberds' cottage was cosy in its way. Crowded but cosy. And cottage was a rather grand name for a tar-covered timber shack. It had been built by Reuben's father when Reuben was a baby.

There was another baby now, called Francis, and Reuben was his uncle, which made Reuben feel grown-up and peculiar at the same time. Francis was only three months old but was cheerful and didn't cry a lot. This was lucky because the cottage was really one big room, with stairs to an open attic, so when he did cry there was no escape from the noise. Apart from Francis and Reuben, three other people lived in the cottage: Reuben's grandfather, who was called Grampy; Reuben's older brother Daniel; and Daniel's wife Molly.

Reuben's parents were both dead. His mother had died in childbirth many years ago, and Reuben barely remembered her. His father had drowned only last year. He'd been a fisherman, like Reuben's brother Daniel. His boat had been lost with him, and Daniel had only recently finished building a new one, so the winter had been even harder and hungrier than usual. The neighbours helped as much as they could: the Olivers were generous people. Everything about them was big: their hearts, their cottage, their family, and especially Bull Oliver himself. Bull was a fisherman too but that wasn't why his wife, Dinah, and their six children never went hungry. Fish, as Bull put it, were too slippery to depend on. So he used his fishing boat for other business as well. Secret business.

Dinah was at Reuben's shoulder now as he stood

4

at the rough table in the backyard, hurriedly plucking the dead razorbills and guillemots. He didn't like the ripping noise as the feathers came out. Molly usually did this job, she was much quicker at it, but Molly was feeding Francis.

'I'll take the lot,' said Dinah, meaning the plucked carcases.

Reuben looked at her.

'Bull's putting down some extra pots,' she said, 'so he needs more bait.'

Reuben knew she was just being kind. The crab and lobster season was well past its peak despite the cold spring. No one was putting down extra pots.

Dinah thrust sixpence into Reuben's hand and swept the dumpy little carcases into her basket before he could argue. Rain was staining the wooden table now. Dinah raised her head to the sea and the weather, then squinted up towards Grampy, who could be seen tottering against the clifftop gale.

'And p'raps the storm'll bring you more than sixpence,' she said.

Grampy lay full length on the clifftop grass. He held the telescope steady, despite the wind and rain that whipped across him, and tried to focus. He could see the ship more clearly by the second. She'd been too slow to shorten sail and now those

5

sails were being torn away, while the ship itself was being turned slowly, inexorably, broadside towards the storm. Another half an hour and she'd be on the rock ledge at the mouth of Cormorant Bay. It was still hard to tell what she was exactly: merchantman or man-of-war. Grampy hoped fervently that she was a merchantman, because that meant a cargo, and cargo on the shore was what the beach-dwellers longed for.

Deep in the lower hold of the distant ship, a small boy sat huddled in the darkness. His name was Pin. He had thought it wouldn't take very long to get to India, not on a ship with so many sails.

He didn't actually know where India was but he'd liked the look of it in the pictures he'd seen. He'd particularly liked the look of the banquets the kings ate there, sitting on silk cushions. And the palm trees. And the elephants. Pin wanted so much to ride an elephant. And the big thing was, it was hot in India. He'd heard a soldier say that. Pin had lost a toe to frostbite in London last winter. No fear of frostbite in India. Or on this ship. He'd been full of confidence and excitement when he'd shinned up the dockside mooring rope. A boy who could do that without being spotted by the crew could surely find himself enough to eat once on board. And stay snug and hidden all the way. But he wasn't feeling snug any more, he was feeling threatened. Threatened by the ship's cargo into which he'd so eagerly burrowed.

A short while ago, the ship had begun to shudder. Then the shuddering had changed to loud banging: a succession of plunging collisions that grew more frequent, so that the crates around Pin shifted and then began to tumble, tossed like giant dice in the creaking dark. Pin fearfully dodged the lethal crates, pressing himself against the wall of the hold, but he knew it was only a matter of time before he was crushed. He must get out. He realized the ship had encountered rough seas. Surely the crew would be too busy with their ropes and sails to notice if he emerged on deck? There must be somewhere he could hide in the open until the hold became safe again.

He climbed towards the hatch and pushed it. Nothing happened. He heaved again without success, then heard the cargo sliding and falling in the upper hold, as it was in his own. A crate must have jammed across the hatch. He was trapped. Trapped like a rat. And like a rat, he scrabbled at the rough, unyielding barrier above his head, ignoring the splinters that drew blood beneath his fingernails.

Suddenly, the motion of the ship changed again, throwing him away from the hatch, and Pin sensed something unnatural in the way the vessel was now being shouldered by the sea, sideways on. Then he heard the shriek. An inhuman noise, filling the hold as the ship's keel scraped, agonized, across the jaws of a reef. The ship lurched briefly upright before the planking beneath Pin's feet ruptured and icy cold water washed in around him, hissing and gurgling as it rose swiftly towards the low rafters above him.

Pin fought his way through the now floating cargo and reached the hatch again at the same moment as the seawater. He was briefly submerged, but whatever had blocked the hatch earlier had shifted again and he burst into the upper hold as the water forced him through, like a cork from a bottle. The sea boiled up after Pin as he floundered onwards. If the main hatch had been battened on the outside against the storm, he was dead. But to his relief, it opened.

Thankfully, Pin climbed out into the world of air and light, only to be knocked instantly from his feet by a wave that swept the deck and crashed him hard against the ship's bulwark. He clung on, half drowned, half unconscious, as the sudden deafening nightmare of wind and sea, torn sails and helpless, terrified men revolved around him.

A sailor, trying desperately to secure himself to the nearest mast, stared a moment at Pin, then the keel shrieked again, the ship lurched, and the man slithered away past him, snatching vainly at

Pin's arm before disappearing over the side with a scream that Pin saw rather than heard.

A moment later the next wave to mount the deck engulfed Pin himself and dragged his fingers free, washing him overboard before surging on towards the surf-lined shore.

Reuben turned from tickling Francis as the back door of the cottage burst open and Grampy appeared.

'Merchantman grounded!' cried the rain-soaked old man. 'And she'll not escape!'

The rest of the Hibberds quickly followed him outside. There was a large crowd already on the beach. The entire Oliver family was there, but also farmhands, carpenters, ditch-diggers, almost the whole scattered village, drawn by word of mouth from those who, like Grampy, had first seen the possibility of a wreck.

Reuben could feel the tension around him as the crowd watched in silence, eager but anxious, willing the stricken ship towards them. Then a great cheer went up, a cheer for the wind and sea, and for the mighty wave that finally wrenched the ship from her lopsided perch on the ledge. Now she would be theirs. Now there was nothing to stop her being driven to them by the onshore wind.

Reuben glanced at Daniel and Molly close beside him. Daniel gave a rueful little shrug. He was a father himself now. He understood the desperate need to clothe and feed a family.

'Come on, my girl!' bellowed Bull Oliver at the wallowing, sinking ship. 'Closer now! Closer! Don't be shy!'

And in response, another huge wave lifted the ship high and carried her broadside-on towards the beach, as if she were a gift.

Reuben closed his eyes as the wave crashed and the ship's hull scraped and rolled in the surf like a dead thing. The following wave righted the ship but drove her deeper into the sea-beach, where she stuck fast, and a roar of triumph around Reuben announced that the gift had been delivered. As he opened his eyes, the crowd was already jostling past: men, women and children, desperate for their share of what the ship's disintegrating holds might offer.

'Move yourself then, nipper!'

Grampy already had the end of Reuben's cliff rope fastened round his own waist. He thrust the rest of the coil at Reuben then sat down heavily.

'Hurry, or they land crabs'll take the lot!'

Reuben dashed into the sea, knotting the other end of the rope round him as he went. The line, with Grampy as anchor, gave him an advantage. He might be knocked over by the breaking surf but didn't fear being washed away. All around him, squeals of excitement were changing to sudden frightened shouts as fellow plunderers were dragged from their feet by the undertow and reduced to clawing their way back to shore on all fours, like survivors of the wreck itself.

Survivors. Were there any? She was a good-sized ship: three masts, two of them broken as she'd rolled in the surf before coming to rest. She must have a crew of more than twenty, and none were to be seen.

Reuben was swallowed by a towering wave, and as he clung to his rope amid the swirling roar of water, something banged into him. The wave surged on up the beach and as Reuben staggered, choking, to his feet again, he saw through stinging eyes that he'd been hit by a body. It lay lifeless on its back beside him, its mouth and eyes gaping. Then the spent wave retreated, dragging at the lifeless body as it went, sucking it back into the deep.

'Grab him!' roared Grampy from the beach, the rope taut in his hands.

And Reuben dug his heels into the sliding shingle and clung to the corpse.

Pin lost his grip on the wooden crate as it was smashed against the rocks. It had been his friend since soon after he'd been washed from the ship but now it left him. All around, other crates and bales were being thrown up by the waves, then carried off again. Pin kicked and threshed, trying to grab hold of something, anything, to help him keep afloat, but the nearest crate ducked and slid away from him. And the rocks, when he was close enough, were too slippery. His strength was failing fast now, and he was choking on seawater.

Then he saw people edging along the base of the cliff towards him, dodging the furious seas. They were coming for him. Risking their lives to rescue him! He tried to wave an arm and shout, but they ignored him and began dragging a wooden crate from the sea instead. They struggled back with it the way they'd come and others did the same: seeing and ignoring him, rescuing the crates. Then a boy of about his own age paused and looked straight at him.

Pin raised both arms and cried out, but could not prevent himself from disappearing, exhausted, beneath the next wave. The last thing he saw was the boy, still hesitating. He knew he was drowning now. He'd fought his hardest but could fight no more. Great fronds of seaweed furled gently round him. He was sorry he would never ride an elephant.

The sudden thump of the waves on the cliff came as a shock, as did the shower of spray. Pin coughed and retched as fingernails tore his shirt, scrabbling at him before gripping him by the armpit and hauling him on to the rocks, where he lay gasping and staring, like a stranded fish.

The boy standing over him returned the stare for a moment. Then he seemed to panic, and ran away.

2

Blue-Coats

Reuben was appalled by what he'd done. He hurried back to the beach empty-handed, slipping and scrambling across the rocks, oblivious to the drenching spray. He could tell by the glances and mutterings as he passed that others had seen and were appalled too.

The boy would still die, Reuben told himself. The waves would wash him off again. He'd perish in the cold. A rock would fall on him. But it didn't help; the deed was done. He'd rescued someone from the sea. Broken the pact. The sea provided a living, of a kind, but in return it took life when it chose. That was the bargain. That was why so few sailors and fishermen ever learnt to swim. Why his father hadn't. Or Grampy. You let the sea decide; you didn't try to cheat it. Certainly, you never rescued a stranger. For if you did, the sea would take you, or one of your family, in place of the person you had saved.

'What was that you found?' asked Grampy, frowning, as Reuben reached him.

'Nothing,' mumbled Reuben, trying to avoid the old man's eyes.

'And nothin's what you've come back with,' grumbled Grampy. 'Look sharp and help me here.'

He'd claimed two crates and Reuben helped him drag them from the water's edge. Grampy used the iron cliff spike to break the first one open.

'Oranges?' asked Reuben hopefully. There had been oranges once, thousands of them, bubbling up from a wrecked Spanish brig. He'd longed ever since to taste another one. The thought took his mind off the rescue for a moment.

'Buttons,' grunted his grandfather, throwing the lid of the crate aside. 'Buttons, buttons, buttons . . .'

He ran his fingers through the rather boring treasure. The buttons were of brass, sturdy and useful, but Reuben shared his grandfather's lack of enthusiasm.

Grampy shuffled on his knees to the next crate and prised that open too. The contents were tightly bound in oilcloth. Grampy used his clasp knife to cut the cords and pulled open the cloth, then stopped.

'Fetch the handcart,' he said, without looking up.

Peering over his shoulder, Reuben glimpsed the spotless steel barrels of a dozen rifles before Grampy swiftly covered them again.

'Fetch the handcart,' repeated Grampy, his voice sharp.

Reuben ran off along the beach to the cottage, passing a steady stream of Oliver children as he went. At times like this there seemed more like twenty-six of them than six. They scuttled back and forth along the sand, crouched and watchful beneath their burdens, disappearing briefly into their cottage then returning for more, marshalled all the time by the busy Dinah. Trousers and tunics, boots, bottles, spades, pickaxes, anything they could carry, was quickly stowed away. Soon Bull himself would be on board the ship with his axe, felling the remaining mast. Then he would start on the deck timbers. Nobody could strip a wreck like the Olivers. If they were land crabs, as everyone called them, the rest of the scavengers on the beach, even the Hibberds, were mere sea lice.

When Reuben returned with the handcart, Grampy had resealed the crate of rifles and collected a heap of the glossy wet kelp dumped by the high tide.

'Take it up the Nest,' he said, as between them they heaved the crate on to the handcart and covered it with kelp.

Reuben didn't need telling twice. He knew the rifles were valuable and must be hidden. He forced the creaking, wobble-wheeled cart into motion and ploughed away with it, heading west towards the high chalk of the headland, the Cormorant Cliff. Now the tide was ebbing, there would be a way up from the shore with the cart about half a mile past the cottages.

'Seaweed for Farmer Toogood,' was his prepared answer, should he be asked what he was transporting. But nobody was likely to enquire: people preferred not to know too much, or had other ways of finding out. As he pushed and sweated, he glanced across to the far side of the bay but couldn't see the boy on the rocks. Perhaps that was only because he didn't want to.

Pin lay quite still for several minutes. No one came near him after his strange rescuer had gone, but he could hear the sea retreating a little, and the wind and rain easing. He had survived.

At length, he sat up and saw that he was completely alone on the rocks. Then he saw the wrecked ship. People were climbing on to it. Others were running about collecting what they could of the strewn cargo. Two of them were pulling a body from the surf. They seemed to be fighting over it. Eventually the victor spreadeagled the body on the sand and removed its jacket. Pin shivered. And not just from the cold.

The Nest was a hole in the hillside behind a clump of elder trees and a nettle bed. Reuben was just replacing the bracken that covered it when he heard hooves. Not a carthorse, more like cavalry travelling fast. He dragged the handcart with him into the nettles and crouched down as the horsemen thundered by on the nearby track: a leader on a black horse, then six others. They wore blue jackets and hats, and red bandanas round their necks. Reuben saw pistols in their belts. And swords. They urged their horses up over the shoulder of the down towards the chalk cliffs. Alarmed but curious, Reuben stealthily followed.

Their leader reined in his horse as close to the cliff edge as he dared. The entire sweep of Cormorant Bay was below him. He could see the ship, or what was left of it. The one remaining mast was sail-less and only one horizontal spar was still in place, giving the mast the appearance of a stark giant cross rising above the distant surf. It was a melancholy sight, made worse by the locals, swarming over and round the wreck. Their behaviour was disgusting, profane. The urge to drive them all into the sea and drown them like rats was almost irresistible. He drew his sword and turned.

'Your first action, boys,' he announced. 'Let us set a swift example.'

'Aye, sir!' cried his men, as one.

And they followed the black horse excitedly as it was spurred away; while behind them, Reuben scrambled back down through the twisted blackthorn bushes and ran for home.

Pin had watched four bodies dragged above the tideline. The man who'd taken the jacket had left his corpse, but a group of children had scampered up to it and hauled it away. Pin supposed if he hadn't been rescued by the boy, he too would have been washed up dead by now and laid next to the other neatly arranged corpses. He'd seen dead bodies before, of course, in London. And he'd seen looting. It was the thoroughness in this place that unnerved him. Nothing, it seemed, would be wasted.

He began to move a little closer, but as he did so, something hit him on the chest. A rock. He ducked just in time as another glanced off his head, and the throwing didn't stop until he retreated.

Pin was bewildered. He hoped the boy would come back. If he did, it might be different. He could see him now, running along the beach with an empty handcart. But he was heading towards the wreck.

Grampy was standing beneath the prow, gazing up at the figurehead. She was a black-haired woman. Her face was brown, though the paint was chipped, and her red mouth was open. Her large eyes stared up at the dismal boggy cliff, as if unable to comprehend that she had been brought low in such a place. She had graced the oceans of the world, carried exotic cargoes, and now ended her days in humiliation.

Grampy felt sorry for her. There was no sentiment in survival; he seized what the sea offered as eagerly as the next man. But the death of a ship always saddened him. Her name was the *Calicut*. He knew Calicut was a spice port in India. He'd been there once, long ago.

Perhaps the ship had been on her way there now. Certainly from her cargo, she was outward bound – full of supplies for some colony or other.

'Grampy! There's men with guns and swords!'

Grampy turned, startled. Reuben had arrived in a lather, lungs bursting.

'What?'

'Coming down off Cormorant on horses!'

Grampy frowned. 'Customs men?'

'Don't think so,' gasped Reuben. 'Proper uniforms.'

'Soldiers?' asked Grampy, sharply. 'Army?'

Reuben didn't know.

'You're goin' daft, nipper,' said Grampy.

He turned dismissively away, only to see the group of blue-coated horsemen arrive on the cliff above the ladder.

'Secure the ship and cargo!' ordered Lieutenant Cade.

The patrol dismounted swiftly, climbed down the ladder with the ease of trained sailors, then crunched across the shingle, swords and pistols drawn.

Lieutenant Cade watched approvingly as one by one the wreckers on the beach dropped what they were taking when confronted by his blue-coats. Then he coaxed the great horse forward, staying expertly upright in the saddle as his mount plunged and slid down through the mud and rock rubble of the cliff.

Bull Oliver was on the ship. He saw the blue-coats coming but ignored them.

'Come down off there!'

Bull ignored the shout as well, and went on hacking at the forward rigging with his axe. He didn't see the pistol raised and aimed, but he heard the shot well enough, and the splintering of wood from the mast just above his head.

The gunshot caused panic and a hurried disembarkation by everyone except Bull himself, who turned and coolly regarded the blue-coat who had fired it.

'Who are you then?' he asked.

'Boatman Gibbs. Coastguard.'

'Coastguard?' grunted Bull. 'Don't need *our* coast guarding, boy. We does that ourselves.' And he resumed his work on the wreck.

'This ship's still the property of its owner,' said

Boatman Gibbs. 'And the cargo belongs to His Majesty's Army. The next shot's in the back of your head. Get off.'

He cocked his second pistol and started counting. He'd given the man fair warning; when he reached ten he'd give him the hole in the skull he seemed to want. Boatman Gibbs had fought pirates in the Mediterranean; insolent tide-waders with blunt axes, like this man here, didn't worry him.

There was a ripple in the gathering crowd to his left and an old salt pushed through, hopping on one foot. A young boy was with him.

'Come on, Bull,' said the old salt. 'You already got enough rope and wood to build a navy.'

Bull seemed to take no notice, then suddenly hurled his axe down on to the wet sand, and immediately launched himself after it, landing heavily in front of Gibbs, and slowly straightening up to his full, overbearing height. But the pistol followed his forehead all the way.

'Thank you,' said Boatman Gibbs, disappointed that he'd only got to nine. 'Now you can all go home.'

'Wait!'

The voice behind the blue-coats was sharp and used to obedience. The muttering crowd obeyed, staring up at the rider of the imposing black horse.

'We should introduce ourselves properly,

boatman. It's only polite.' He raised his hat. 'Lieutenant Cade, formerly of His Majesty's Navy, now Chief Officer of the newly formed Coastguard, here to enforce the King's peace and justice on this small but significant stretch of our nation's shore.'

His gaze moved slowly over the ignorant, ill-assorted faces. They returned his look impassively, though whether their stares were defiant or merely vacant, Lieutenant Cade couldn't tell.

'By the King's peace and justice,' he continued, 'I mean the laws of property and revenue.' He smiled. 'But there is no need for alarm. Regard me not as a tyrant, but a teacher, come to educate you out of two mistaken beliefs.'

Very few in the crowd had been to school. All were intrigued that a teacher should carry a sword and pistols.

'The first belief,' said Lieutenant Cade, 'is that anything that has been washed in salt water is somehow in need of a new owner. But I must tell you that to carry off such goods is not innocent acceptance of "the sea's bounty". It is theft.'

Bull Oliver spat on the sand, but other members of the crowd studied the sky or their feet.

'The second belief is that the secret importation of brandy, tea, lace and tobacco without payment of tax is innocent "free trade". It is not. It is smuggling. And smuggling is also theft.'

23

Lieutenant Cade paused, then straightened in the saddle and smiled again.

'Learn these lessons well and we shall be friends. Continue in your old ways and we shall not. But understand that if we are not friends, you shall find me a far more dangerous enemy than the idle and corrupt officers of Customs who formerly patrolled your coast. Or pretended to. For I am neither idle nor corrupt. And nor are my men.'

He nodded once, and within seconds the patrol had formed up into a solid blue unit. Disciplined, orderly. For Lieutenant Cade would have order. He'd had it on board His Majesty's ships, and he meant to show these sullen, lawless ruffians that he would have it here on their beach as well.

'Any person who approaches the ship,' he said, no longer smiling, 'will be shot. As will any person who touches what remains of the cargo. The corpses you may dispose of in the appropriate manner.'

Lieutenant Cade had meant to finish there, but his distaste, his disappointment, were too strong.

'Is there one of you here who is not English?' he asked. 'Are you not all sons and daughters of our noble and victorious nation? We have crushed Napoleon Bonaparte, who would have subjected all of Europe to his tyranny. New horizons beckon every day. And yet here are you, picking and pecking like carrion crows on a dead cow. Where is your pride?'

'It starved last winter.'

Lieutenant Cade turned slowly to identify the source of the quiet reply. It came from the old man with one foot. Probably a sailor. Old enough to have served with Lord Nelson. Lieutenant Cade felt a brief prickle of self-reproach but shook it off. Poverty was an excuse for criminality, not a reason.

'We'll have the cargo stacked, if you please,' he said to his men. 'Fall out.'

The next moment, Boatman Gibbs was on his face in a pool of grey mud and the crowd was trying, though not successfully, to suppress a roar of laughter. Gibbs struggled to his feet and hurled himself at Bull Oliver, who had tripped him. Daniel got between them and Grampy grabbed Bull as the other blue-coats intervened.

'Stop that!' shouted Lieutenant Cade, riding into the scuffle.

The two men had been quickly separated, Gibbs glaring balefully as he spat out mud, Bull Oliver grinning back at him.

Bull looked up at Lieutenant Cade and shrugged.

'You said fall out,' he explained. 'I was only helpin' him.'

Lieutenant Cade stared down.

'What's your name?' he demanded.

'Oliver.'

Lieutenant Cade continued to stare, then turned to Boatman Gibbs as if nothing had happened.

'The cargo, if you please, boatman. And two on sentry.'

He backed his horse carefully out of the crowd and departed. As he rode towards the low cliff by the ladder, he heard someone running behind him and started to draw his sword.

A hand touched his stirrup and Lieutenant Cade reared his horse round, ready to strike. A small boy was gazing fearfully up at him, a ragged urchin, dodging the hooves.

'Please, sir,' he cried, 'I'm off the ship – will you take me with you?'

He looked no different from the rest. Lieutenant Cade didn't even bother to reply.

'It's unjust!' Bull Oliver's great fist thumped the table.

'It's the law,' said his wife, sucking on her pipe. 'As you well know. Difference now is it seems likely to be enforced.' She sniffed, unperturbed. 'For a while.'

'Coastguards!' roared Bull with contempt. 'Well, they better guard themselves first!'

He would have paced his parlour floor but it was too full of people.

'You touch 'em again and you'll swing,' said Dinah.

'Me swing?' laughed Bull. 'The gallows ain't built that's strong enough.'

'Then they'll build one, my boy. Forget it. Forget the wreck. Your family's new clothed and booted, ain't it? Then be content.'

Bull was not content. He glowered at his wife.

'Wrecks are not the main business,' insisted Dinah. 'Wrecks are a nuisance to them, just as they're a blessing to us.' She relit her pipe from the fire and blew smoke at a ship's compass, one of many adorning the walls. 'It's the trade we must be careful of. It's the trade they mean to stop.'

'They'd find it easier to stop the tide,' grunted Bull savagely.

His defiance found a loud enthusiastic echo in the crowded fug. Reuben was aware of Grampy joining in; and of Daniel remaining silent. He knew his brother never got involved in smuggling – 'the trade', as it was called – and this sometimes disappointed him. It was a dangerous business, especially the secret landing of brandy from France, but there was always a ready market for such goods because they were cheap.

Even respectable people like Squire Coleman and Parson Teague bought from the smugglers. Even educated men like Mr Pocock, who also bought dead seabirds from Reuben, paid for a share. It was illegal but it was part of life on the coast and almost everyone, rich and poor, was involved. Except Daniel. For if caught, he knew he would be imprisoned, or worse, and without him, only Reuben would be left to keep his wife and baby. Daniel never said as much to Grampy, but both he and the old man knew it was true, because Grampy could no longer climb in and out of a fishing boat.

Bull Oliver had no such problems. He was a smuggler and meant to go on smuggling. 'They don't frighten me with their pistols and fancy blue uniforms!'

'Bull,' said Dinah, not for the first time in their married life, 'you're talking fish guts.'

'We have a right to live, don't we?' shouted Bull.

He banged the table again and several dead sea captains' teacups rattled in their saucers.

'We do,' said Dinah calmly. 'But we must be careful now. *You* must be careful. And not behave as if you had the brains of a lobster.'

Bull suddenly lunged forward, and for an instant Reuben thought he would strike his wife, but no, his keen ears had heard something outside. He charged straight past Dinah to the door and yanked it open.

Reuben heard a sharp cry and instantly felt his face burning and his mouth going dry.

'Who's this then?' demanded Bull, turning to the room with a small boy dangling from his fist.

'Best ask Reuben,' said Dinah, without mercy.

Bull looked towards Reuben, uncomprehending, fierce. The room was hushed.

'I'm sorry, Bull,' said Reuben lamely. 'I don't know why I did it . . .'

His croaking voice then failed him altogether.

'Reuben fished him from the sea,' explained Dinah bluntly. 'You've got bad luck in your hands.'

Bull reacted as if stung, flinging Pin outside and slamming the door.

'You did *what*?' he shouted.

Reuben felt Grampy's hand clutch his shoulder protectively as others confirmed what Dinah said. Daniel stepped in front of Reuben as Bull moved angrily towards him.

'Leave the boy alone, Bull,' he said. 'There's no harm done.'

'Yet.'

The interruption was cold and cynical. Reuben recognized Asher's voice. Another fisherman. He was wearing a sea captain's jacket that Reuben hadn't seen him in before.

'It ain't only about taking what's rightfully the sea's, Daniel. There's the trade too. 'Tis all very well for you to say no harm's done: you who takes as little risk as possible.'

Daniel tried not to react to the sly taunt.

'I think I know the code as well as anyone,' he said. 'But you can't expect a child to be entirely ruthless, Asher. He must learn that from his betters such as you.'

Reuben blushed deeper still at being referred to as a child and needing his eighteen-year-old brother to defend him.

'Bad luck's bad luck,' said Dinah firmly, not wanting fisticuffs in her parlour. 'However innocent it comes. And we've enough already with these blue-coats come upon us. I shan't invite more, not in my house.' She jerked her head at the closed door and the small saved boy beyond it. 'You may throw him back or feed him as you wish, Daniel. But he don't come near me or mine.'

The entire parlour growled agreement. Reuben felt he had turned the world against his family.

Pin sprang away from the cottage door as it opened and watched, hidden in the darkness, as those inside filed out.

He'd heard enough to understand his rescue was the cause of his rejection. He was tired, starved, frozen. And lost. The sentries at the far end of the beach had lit a small fire, but Pin knew he'd get no better welcome there. Instead, when the door had closed again and all was quiet, he crept past both cottages to the rough shelter beyond, and made himself a sleeping hole among the lobster pots and nets.

'Is that you in there?'

The question was cautious rather than abrupt, but Pin didn't answer. He tried not to breathe. He thought he heard someone walking away, but he couldn't be sure against the noise of the sea. Then the footsteps returned slowly across the sliding pebbles. A hovering light danced on the wicker pots around Pin, then a candle was being shielded right in front of his eyes. It was held by the boy who'd rescued him.

'You can come indoors,' he said.

Pin shook his head vigorously.

'They say it's all right. My family.'

'No,' said Pin, suddenly more proud than sensible. 'I don't want to. You done enough.'

His rescuer seemed uncertain but eventually turned away. Pin's stomach instantly regretted his decision and rumbled accusingly but he ignored it and tried to make himself comfortable.

Then, after a while, the footsteps and candle returned. The boy from the cottage was carrying a platter now. He didn't speak, just emptied the contents on to Pin's lap and went away again. Floury cold potato had never tasted so good.

Reuben had kept one potato for himself. He sat at the table, eating it in silence, and fervently hoping that the boy would be gone by morning.

The crash woke Pin and frightened him. For a second, the tightness of his makeshift bed between

31

the pots and the close roaring of the sea made him think he was aboard the ship. Then he saw a lantern, and the cottage door collapsing inwards.

Indoors, Reuben leapt to his feet as the door caved in. He too thought the sea had reached the cottage, but the sea had boots and smelt of sweat and was shouting. A rough hand grabbed him and pushed him against the wall, holding him fast as a lantern was flashed in his face.

'Don't move!' ordered a voice as rough as the hand.

More boots and lanterns trampled and swayed in past Reuben and his captor, and as they spread through the cottage like a flood, their leader loomed, smiling in the doorway behind them. And Reuben came face to face with Lieutenant Cade.

3

The Broken Net

The house search was thorough and destructive. It discovered nothing but that was not the point. Lieutenant Cade did not really expect to find barrels of brandy or bales of tobacco or lace hidden in the cottage. Smugglers were not that stupid. And anything from the wreck worth his attention would also have been squirrelled away by now. But smugglers and wreckers should know his power. He could intrude and turn their homes and lives upside down whenever he chose, night or day. He would hound them all, wear them down until they lost the will to defy the law and its enforcers.

Reuben had been thrown in among the rest of his family at the foot of the stairs, and stood supporting Grampy, whose stick had been lost in the tumult. Beside him, Daniel clenched his fists helplessly and Molly shushed Francis in her arms, while Boatman Gibbs held a pistol pointed at the tight little group. Above their heads the thin ceiling creaked and bumped under the heavy tread of blue-coats in the attic bedroom.

Reuben heard a cupboard overturn, then something smash. Francis began to cry. Then bedding was strewn down the open staircase and the blue-coats trampled over it as they returned to the ground floor. One of them shook his head at Lieutenant Cade, who nodded politely at the family as if he'd been entertained to tea, and strolled out.

'The boats, and then next door,' he ordered.

Mention of the boats made Daniel hurry after them in alarm. He must protect his livelihood, even if he couldn't protect his home. But the moment he'd gone, Molly turned to Reuben, her voice a panicked whisper.

'Reuben – I left two boxes outside yesterday, when Francis woke. They'll know they're from the wreck!'

Reuben stared in dismay but he squeezed Molly's arm.

'Don't worry.' And he ran to the back of the cottage and out into the yard.

Pin had crept from among the lobster pots while the blue-coats were in the cottage. Now, as they reappeared and lantern light spilt across the beach, he saw two boats, one larger than the other, drawn up close by, and something propped against the smaller boat: a pair of wooden boxes, small, sturdy, with black printing on them. Pin had seen something similar on the beach the day before. Perhaps the blue-coats were searching for them now.

The lanterns halted briefly as the blue-coats stooped to pick up what looked like long sticks, and in that moment Pin decided what to do.

As Reuben paused in the shadow of the cottage wall, preparing to lunge out and try to scoop up the boxes unseen, he saw Pin dive from the shelter a few paces away. Whisking the boxes with him, the small boy vanished into the darkness beneath the dank bushes at the bottom of the cliff.

The boxes tucked behind him, Pin crouched and watched the blue-coats march forward and drive their iron-spiked poles into the fishing nets heaped and draped across the boats. He heard shouting from behind the blue-coats. People had come out of the boy's cottage and the one next door.

Boatman Gibbs paid no attention to the noise. He jabbed vigorously at the thick mound of damp netting in the smaller boat, entirely careless of the damage he might cause.

'Tear my nets and we shall starve!' cried Daniel, running towards him.

'Your stomach's in less danger than your neck,' replied Boatman Gibbs.

He kept jabbing with the spike, though clearly there was nothing hidden beneath the net, until Daniel grabbed him by the shoulder and pulled him from the boat.

'Stand away!' ordered Lieutenant Cade, and Daniel was instantly surrounded and restrained, only to break free again and plunge his hands into the fishing net, dragging a fold of it towards the lantern light to show a great tear in the mesh.

'Is this how you "educate" us?' he shouted at Lieutenant Cade. 'By breaking one law to enforce another? By trespass and wanton damage? By destroying our means of an honest living!'

'The net was already torn,' lied Boatman Gibbs, unconcerned.

Lieutenant Cade looked at Daniel and shrugged.

'If you claim to be a fisherman,' he said calmly, 'no doubt you will be able to mend it.'

And he turned away from the Hibberds and then past Bull and Dinah, to search their home at gunpoint too.

Reuben had forgotten Pin for the moment in the angry clash over the net, and now he brought a candle to help Daniel inspect the net more thoroughly. With each broken mesh discovered, his brother's fury and frustration grew, so that Reuben was quite relieved when eventually the wind blew out the candle and they had to stop.

As they turned towards the cottage, they heard a movement, then a voice, as Pin emerged.

'Them boxes,' he whispered. 'I hid 'em in the bushes.'

Daniel looked at Reuben.

'Boxes?'

Molly had emerged from the cottage now and she quickly explained, but Daniel said nothing more. It wasn't like him to brood but the violence of the raid and his powerlessness to stop it had affected him deeply. There was certainly a difference between the new coastguards and the old Customs men, and to Daniel the difference was mere brutality and injustice. Besides, although the meagre contents of the cottage could be put back together after a fashion, his fishing net was another matter.

In the morning, when they retrieved the boxes from the bushes, they found they contained rifle ammunition, and there was relief that they hadn't been caught in possession of such a dangerous piece of salvage. Molly was even more grateful for Pin's quick thinking than before and rewarded him in the best possible way – with breakfast.

Pin ate as much as he was offered, perhaps a little more; he felt he'd repaid at least part of his debt to the boy called Reuben, and to his family.

The inside of their house smelt of tar and fish and rotten potatoes, but it was good to be indoors again. The woman was kind and the old man was talkative, but the boy didn't say much. He was sitting on the step outside the broken door, helping the older brother mend his fishing net.

'What's your name then, nipper?' asked Grampy.

'Pin. I'm called Pin.'

Reuben laughed. 'Is that a proper name?'

Pin looked across at him. 'It's a London name,' he said. 'It's cos I'm small and sharp.'

It was true that he'd always been called Pin because he was small. Sharp was his own addition. He was growing in confidence with every mouthful of bread.

'And how was you on the ship, then?' asked Grampy.

'Passenger,' said Pin. 'I've got family in India. They sent for me.'

Grampy regarded the boy's ragged clothes but didn't comment.

'A rare place, India,' he said, nodding. 'And when was you to get there?'

'Next week,' said Pin, blithely through his bread.

Reuben looked up from the net again. He wasn't sure himself how long it took to get to India but knew it was a lot longer than a week, even in the fastest ship. His eyes met Grampy's but Grampy shook his head just slightly. He found Pin's fibs entertaining and didn't want them interrupted.

'What port then?' he asked.

Pin pondered while he swallowed. 'Kingston.'

Reuben snorted. Kingston wasn't in India; it was in the West Indies. When he glanced up again, Pin was chewing unconcernedly on another hunk of bread. If he knew his barefaced lies had been detected, he wasn't concerned. Reuben didn't like that much. Why not tell the truth? Especially when you were eating someone else's food.

Grampy was examining the contents of the wooden boxes again, more thoroughly now. He plucked out one of the paper-covered cartridges and rolled it between finger and thumb. Still dry. Not spoilt by the sea.

'Best get these up the Nest as well, Reuben,' he said. 'If you can spare him, Daniel?'

'I can spare him,' replied Daniel, preoccupied. He knew mackerel had been sighted further down the coast and needed the net mended quickly. But Reuben's fingers, though willing, weren't yet strong enough for the needle and twine. 'Don't forget the bodies,' he added, without looking up.

Pin jumped down eagerly from the table.

'I'll carry one o' them boxes, shall I?'

'No, I can manage,' said Reuben, with a hasty shake of the head.

The London boy's blatant lies about the ship and India may have amused Grampy but Reuben wasn't going to trust him. Most likely, he thought, he was a runaway thief. But before Reuben could hurry away on his own, Gums arrived.

Gums was the shepherd from Toogood's Farm and had brought a horse and wagon. He'd also brought a rope, and Pin soon realized what it was

39

for: the canvas-covered corpses from the wreck were to be manhandled up the ladder.

'Pin'll help you, nipper,' called Grampy.

Reuben would have protested but his grandfather had already turned away.

'We can't spare you any of the money,' he said sharply, as he waited reluctantly for Pin to join him.

'What money?'

'Cadavers from the sea are worth five shillun each,' said Reuben, heaving from beneath as Gums hauled from above. 'If we give 'em up to Parson Teague for decent burial.'

'Money for the dead?' replied Pin, reacting to Reuben's less than friendly tone. 'I wouldn't touch it, anyway. Bad enough stealin' from a corpse, let alone sellin' it.' He was pleasantly astonished at how pious he could sound.

There were four bodies altogether, and since Bull Oliver refused to profit from them, on the grounds that Lieutenant Cade had said he could, the Hibberds were left with all four: a pound instead of five shillings. But when the wagon was finally loaded, the horse refused to move.

'They're too fresh for 'im,' Gums laughed at Pin. 'He's used to pullin' manure.'

He cackled and dragged the horse forward by its bridle, and Reuben and Pin followed the wagon as it ground its way up the lane towards the church.

Reuben made no effort to speak to Pin, who

after a while forgot his earlier piety and decided to show off.

'In London,' he announced, 'corpses are dug up to be sold, not sold to be buried.'

Reuben did at least look at him.

'Dug up from graveyards,' Pin continued casually. 'Doctors pay for 'em. Learning doctors. They like to cut 'em up to see what's inside. Specially hearts and livers. And brains, o'course.'

Reuben was shocked but tried not to show it.

'How much?' he asked, after a while. 'For a body?'

'Oh, more than five shillins,' said Pin airily. 'A lot more.'

Reuben didn't believe he knew at all.

There was another silence between them, then suddenly the Olivers' land crabs appeared, marching earnestly down the lane past them in a line, all identically dressed in new calico shirts. Pin and Reuben both laughed then glanced at each other and instantly set their faces again.

Parson Teague was away from home as usual, and the sexton had no money to pay the bounty. He was too nervous to have done so if he had: the parson's approval was required, and his signature.

'That's all right,' said Gums, dragging the bodies from the wagon and laying them neatly against the vestry wall. 'You can either bury 'em or talk to 'em. 'Tis all the same to us.'

He took a lump of chalk from beneath the

41

wagon seat and scraped a mark on each of the rough canvas shrouds.

'Just remember: young Reuben's owed a pound for these. Make sure he gets it.' He widened his toothless grin and departed.

Reuben had mixed feelings. He was sorry to go home without his pound but was relieved not to have had to ask Parson Teague for it face to face. Whenever the parson handed over money, whether for smuggled brandy or drowned bodies, he made it seem like he was giving alms to the poor. Reuben was not a beggar.

As he turned for home, he knew full well the London boy was following, and felt a great urge to pick up a stone and hurl it at him, as he would at a nuisance stray dog. But that might get him into trouble with Molly or Grampy.

When he got back to the beach, his heart sank further. Molly had put Reuben's spike and stick with the ammunition boxes.

'Take Pin with you,' she said. 'See how he manages on the cliffs.'

'Why?' exclaimed Reuben, not bothering to lower his voice. 'We don't need him here. We don't *want* him here! We can't afford to keep him!'

'No, no, of course,' said Molly quietly, with a little glance towards Pin, hoping he hadn't heard. 'And I'm sure he'll go soon. But while he's here, he might as well be useful.'

She didn't add that she was concerned that Reuben was getting too heavy for the cliffs. Concerned mostly for his safety but also for the loss of income when a rope would no longer hold his weight. The London boy was pale and puny-looking but she guessed he was agile. She smiled. Reuben sighed and beckoned to Pin.

As the two boys headed away from the cottages, the army arrived: a detachment from the garrison at Sandham. They came with wagons to carry away what cargo the coastguards had managed to gather and had been guarding all night.

Bull Oliver glowered at this further intrusion of uniformed authority, but Daniel barely looked up from the great swathe of fishing net gathered around him.

'The sooner the cargo's gone,' said Daniel, 'the sooner the blue-coats'll leave us in peace.'

'They'll sit on the ship till the owner comes,' grunted Bull. 'I don't call that bein' left in peace.'

Daniel tied off another patch of repaired mesh and tugged at it to test its strength.

'Two good storms and there'll be nothing left to sit on,' he said. 'The owner won't come down to look at driftwood.'

'Two good storms?' Bull was regarding the blue-coat sentries balefully as they went to meet the newly arrived soldiers. 'I can't afford to wait for one.'

*

Reuben insisted that Pin stay well back while he went behind the elder trees and nettle bed and placed the boxes in the Nest. The crate of rifles was still there. Reuben wondered where it might be best to sell a rifle but he didn't mention them to Pin. He wasn't prepared to share any more than he absolutely had to with the newcomer.

The Cormorant Cliff, when Reuben led Pin to its highest point, seemed to excite, not frighten him as Reuben had expected, and hoped. And when Reuben called Pin's bluff and offered him the chance to go down on the rope, he took it, pulling the bag across his shoulder and brandishing the stick as if born to be a cliff boy.

Reuben had a slight qualm as Pin disappeared over the edge, and he drove the spike deeper into the turf to ensure its steadiness. Then he leant over and pointed down, almost to the sea itself.

'That ledge down there,' he called. 'That's the one you want.'

Pin lowered himself on his loop of rope, thrusting himself away from the cliff with his feet, bouncing gently down in the direction Reuben was pointing.

He was not afraid of heights. He'd once been forced to climb a church roof to steal lead – without a rope, at that. And the sea didn't worry him either. It was a brilliant greenish blue today, and calm. He could see all the way to where it merged with the sky. The empty open freshness of this unfamiliar world exhilarated him.

'You've gone past!'

Reuben was yelling down at him. Pin hauled himself up towards the overhanging ledge.

The smell was the first thing that hit him. A stench that literally knocked him backwards, so that he spun, choking, on his rope, then banged helplessly against the rock. Huge black wings spread menacingly before him, and a long hooked beak opened in a featherless face. The bird's leathery webbed feet shifted on its putrid nest: a heap of sticks, liquid droppings and regurgitated fish. Two large chalky-blue eggs lay amid the filth, and writhing between them was a blind and naked nestling, even more repulsive than its parent. The great black bird stared fiercely, then its head darted forward and Pin expected the cruel beak to stab his eyes but instead it struck downwards and appeared to swallow its own young. At which sight, Pin scrabbled away, twisting on his rope as his stomach heaved.

High above him, Reuben laughed as the London boy's breakfast reappeared and sprayed down towards the rocks below.

He was still chortling when he helped Pin back on to the clifftop grass.

'That's a cormorant's nest,' he said. 'Stink, don't they?'

Pin would have hit him but the awful stench was still in his head and he was weak and shaky from being sick. He lay feebly on the ground while Reuben prepared to go down the cliff in his place.

'It was eatin' its little'un,' he said, horrified.

Reuben laughed again. It was his turn to show off now.

'No,' he explained, 'just feeding it. They sort of chew food first then sick it up.'

This didn't make Pin feel better. And he thought he could hear real babies crying now. Human. Lots of them. It was a pitiful sound, quite unlike the noise of the seabirds. He tried to ignore it.

Reuben was still at the cliff edge, standing quite still, gazing out across the bay. Pin hoped he'd lost his nerve. But then Reuben turned suddenly and, to Pin's surprise, grabbed his hand and pulled him to his feet, pointing out to sea at a dark patch on the water and a busy flock of gulls.

'If you really want to help, now's your chance!'

The army was leaving again, its wagons lumbering up the track, and the beach looked swept clean behind them, as Reuben charged towards the ladder.

'Mackerel!' he yelled. 'Mackerel, mackerel!'

He'd left Pin far behind. Every second was vital. He almost fell down the ladder in his haste.

'Mackerel!'

Bull Oliver came running from his cottage, Grampy and Molly appeared, and villagers and fishermen that Reuben had passed on his way were soon arriving.

'Out beyond Chantry Point!' gasped Reuben.

Grampy hopped up the ladder and lurched away towards the southern end of the bay, while the others ran to launch the boats.

'Hurry, Daniel!' roared Bull.

Daniel was still net-mending.

'It's not finished.' He was almost perverse in his anger.

'It'll hold, surely! There's no time for fancy stitchwork.'

Bull turned away to his own boat, quickly but carefully rearranging the net so it would cast cleanly. Others were helping him now, Asher among them, while Reuben and Molly waited fretfully to push the Hibberd boat towards the water. Eventually Daniel threw aside his needle and twine, and dragged his net aboard.

'Where's Pin?' asked Daniel.

'He's far behind,' said Reuben. 'He can help with the landing. Tell him what to do, Molly.'

More men arrived as the boats slid into the rippling surf, but not enough to crew them both, and when Pin appeared on the beach, Daniel gave a shout and waved him forward.

'Quickly, London boy!'

'He can't come in the boat!' cried Reuben.

'He's small, he's quick, we need another hand,' said Daniel.

And he pulled Pin aboard as the boat rose above the first wave, and settled him on the net in the stern, next to Reuben, as he himself took the fourth and final oar.

'Pull, boys, pull then!' cried Bull, and both boats skimmed away towards the frantic mass of wheeling, diving, screeching seagulls, not far offshore now.

Bull looked across at Daniel's boat, laughing, then saw Pin on board and looked away again.

Reuben could feel Bull's deep displeasure but he concentrated on his job, gazing up towards the clifftop at Chantry Point, where Grampy now stood, lurching dangerously close to the edge as he pointed his stick.

'Coming in!' yelled the old man. 'Coming in!'

Reuben peered ahead.

'Ten seconds, Daniel!' he shouted. 'Five!' Then his voice was lost in the shriek of the gulls as both boats veered round so that they were pointing back towards the shore.

'There, Pin!' cried Reuben, forgetting his anxiety and excitedly clutching the London boy's arm. 'D'you see them? Mackerel!'

Pin looked where Reuben was pointing and saw what looked like a huge dark living cloud just below the surface, glinting with a thousand points of blue and silver.

'Help play out the net!'

Pin scrambled up and, watching Reuben closely, helped tumble the fishing net over the stern, where it sank and spread behind the fast-moving boat.

The shoal of fish was between the boats and the shore now, and both sets of oarsmen rowed hard, trying to trap the fish in the shallows. But just as it seemed to Pin that the shoal must swim right on to the beach, the emerald green sea was suddenly whipped and thrashed white, as if by a sudden violent hailstorm, as the fish turned as one and headed back towards deeper water.

'Hold tight!' shouted Reuben. 'It's now or never!'

Pin crouched in the stern, bracing himself, not knowing what to expect. Then the billowing net went taut as the fleeing mackerel swam headlong into it, and the boat recoiled under the weight and pressure of several thousand fish trapped beneath and around it.

'Out now!' ordered Reuben. 'We must help the land crew!'

And he yanked Pin with him over the stern of the boat into shoulder-deep water. Molly and Dinah and half a dozen others had run into the sea now, getting behind the two nets, while others on the shore ran to grab and haul them in.

'Press the net low,' said Reuben, as he and Pin spluttered side by side. 'And mind for rocks or it'll tear and they'll escape.'

Pin grabbed at the net and did his best to hold on, pushing and pressing when Reuben did so; staggering backwards when the squirming, leaping mass inside the net momentarily gained the upper hand.

Both boats were beached now and the oarsmen added their muscle to the struggle to land the catch. The shoal had divided in its bid to escape and each net was equally loaded. Step by step they were dragged from the water, the mackerel hemmed inside fighting more furiously still as they panicked in the suffocating fresh air.

Pin was on his knees, the rainbow colours of the dying fish flashing in futile glory before him. He ignored the countless blank unblinking eyes pressed against the mesh. His lips and eyebrows were now caked with fish scales, and his arms trembled with fatigue, but he clung on. He realized well enough that this was a harvest for the Hibberds. A vital harvest that must not be lost. Never had Pin been so needed, so part of anything. He felt a surge of pride.

Then someone screamed and the net began to part, unravelling in front of him, and he was as helpless as Reuben and the rest to prevent the entire quicksilver mass of fish from slithering and slapping out past him, back into their cold, life-giving home.

Daniel took it badly. The remaining catch was shared generously, but that meant only half as much for everyone who'd taken part. Half as many future days when mackerel, salted and preserved, could be the stand-by supper.

Daniel sat alone outside the cottage while Reuben and Molly instructed Pin in the art of gutting fish. Eventually, Bull approached Daniel and tried to cheer him up. He didn't mention the rescued boy.

'There'll be another catch,' he said heartily. 'The mackerel often come in twice a season.'

'Not these past five years, they haven't,' retorted Daniel.

'You may blame yourself, Daniel,' said Bull. 'You may blame your net-mending. But it's *them* whose fault it truly is.'

He glanced along the beach towards the blue-coat sentries, who still perched watchfully beside the empty wreck.

Daniel nodded but said nothing. Bull sat down carefully beside him.

'Could I hire your boat tonight?' he asked quietly.

Daniel reacted sharply.

'Hire? Your generosity's appreciated, Bull, but not your charity.'

Bull raised a hand. 'No charity. Mine holed when we landed the catch. A day or more's repairing. I need a boat tonight.'

'Why?'

'Why d'you think?' Bull paused, watching Reuben approach, and included him as he continued. 'Actually, if you and Reuben could see your way to come along, I'd be obliged. I've only Asher can join me.' He looked hard at Reuben. 'Though you'll keep that London boy away from it.'

Reuben nodded, though he had no idea as yet what he was agreeing to.

'Only, I must go tonight,' said Bull, 'despite the blue-coats.' He glanced again along the beach. 'The moon and tide's all wrong for days after and the stuff'll turn to stinkibus. Been sunk a month already.' He paused again. 'I pay fair wages, as you know.'

'Aye,' said Daniel, without looking at him.

Bull leant forward. 'Daniel,' he said with quiet urgency, 'there's the law, and there's what's fair and right. As you said to that Lieutenant Cade, what's to be done if they destroy our means of an honest living?'

He placed a hand on Daniel's shoulder.

'It's no mortal sin to help a friend and neighbour, is it?'

Daniel smiled ruefully. 'No,' he said, 'it's not.'

He looked from Bull to Reuben. 'Must Reuben be involved?'

Bull shrugged. 'The more hands we have, the quicker it's done.'

Daniel pondered a moment longer, then nodded and stood up briskly.

'What time do we go?' he asked.

Pin had been given a place to sleep by the potato bin. But the draught beneath the broken door and the reek of mackerel from the buckets all around him eventually persuaded him to creep outside and return to his berth among the lobster pots.

There was no moon and no stars, and he didn't see Daniel and Reuben emerge from the cottage soon afterwards and slip away towards the Cormorant Cliff.

But he heard them. Pin was wide awake and curious. He quickly followed.

4

Black Tooth

Pin was soon lost in a total blackness he'd never known in London. Even the glow of the sentries' pipes had been extinguished: the two blue-coats by the wreck had departed at dusk.

When he started out, Pin could still hear Reuben and Daniel ahead of him, clambering over rocks. Then the rocks became boulders and he gradually lost the sound of their feet. Each time he stopped to listen, he fell further behind, until finally all he could hear, or thought he could hear, was the sea somewhere to his left. Or was it behind him? The boulder he was groping his way over seemed so high that Pin began to wonder if he'd started to climb the cliff. He continued climbing and eventually felt grass beneath his fingers – short, tufty grass, tight as a rug – and realized he *had* climbed the cliff: he'd reached one of the sloping shelves of turf he'd seen when out with Reuben. The going was easier now and soon he reached the top and stood recovering, with a small fresh breeze on his face. Then he saw a light. Brief, yellow, a mere wink in the blackness below to his right.

Reuben was momentarily blinded by the beam as it was pointed straight at him. It came from a spout lantern, a large can with a tube attached, like a watering can. The light inside shone only from the end of the tube and therefore could only be seen in the direction it was pointed. A smuggler's lantern.

'You're late.'

The unwelcoming voice belonged to Asher. The bulk of Bull Oliver loomed beside him.

'Careful with that light, Asher,' said Bull sharply.

Reuben knew the boat must be close by. Bull had rowed it away earlier on his own, so that they didn't all leave the beach together. This was the rendezvous. The very word thrilled him.

Daniel pushed him gently and they followed the other two out on to the slippery rocks at the water's edge.

Reuben could hear the men climbing into the boat, and when his turn came and he scrambled aboard, the spout lantern swung briefly to reveal a jumble of iron hooks, chains and poles in the stern beneath his feet.

As the boat was pushed off and Daniel and Asher unshipped the oars, Bull wedged himself beside Reuben in the stern and picked up a pole with long curved prongs at its end.

'Never met the dragon, have you, nipper?' asked Bull. 'He says good mornin'.' He pulled a cord and chuckled softly as in doing so he made the prongs open and close like fangs in front of Reuben.

Asher and Daniel nudged the boat from among the rocks and rowed silently out across the smooth, ink-black water of the bay. Eventually, they shipped their oars, allowing the boat to drift, and Reuben was required to move so that Bull could lean over the stern, dipping the dragon's jaws into the water and pushing them deep with the pole. He moved the pole gently, as if stirring the sea, then suddenly pulled the cord and levered the pole upwards. Reuben saw the dragon's jaws break the surface.

'Take the weight, nipper,' ordered Bull urgently.

Reuben instantly obeyed, helping to pull the pole back into the boat. It felt heavy now, and as it slid the length of the boat and the jaws came inboard, he saw why. The light from the spout lantern illuminated two glistening wooden tubs, roped together in a kind of sling and weighted with stones.

'Unhook them, Reuben. Quickly.'

Reuben eased the wet rope from the dragon's jaws and, as the tubs clunked together in the bottom of the boat, Bull drove the pole back into the water. The oarsmen dipped their blades to steady the boat and soon Bull was pulling the cord again and heaving the dragon's second catch into the boat. He worked quickly, intently, with Reuben unhooking and stowing the tubs as each pair came inboard.

Then, after several more catches, Bull cursed quietly and turned.

'Too deep for the pole,' he said. 'Are we off the line?'

'No,' said Asher softly. 'Tide's turned.'

Bull passed the dragon pole to Reuben and began to uncoil the chain in the stern.

'Leave it, Bull,' said Asher. 'We got enough.'

'How many?'

'Five pair.'

'There was six pair sunk,' said Bull. 'I'll use the grappler.'

'Leave it! You'll sink us.' Asher's voice was still quiet but angry now. Reuben silently agreed with him. The black water was already close to the boat's gunwale, occasionally slapping cold against his fingers. But Bull ignored the voice, and the chain chinked through his fingers as he dropped the hooked piece of iron attached to it over the stern.

'Sshh!' Asher's voice again, reacting to the noise of the chain and splash of the grappling iron.

Reuben shifted uncomfortably.

'Sshh!' The hissed demand for silence was even fiercer.

Reuben sat very still, suddenly realizing that Daniel, as well as Asher, was doing the same. The raised blades hung motionless above the water. Beside him, Bull strained to keep the chain from rasping against the boat's stern. The spout lantern had been hidden. Everyone was listening, willing themselves invisible and inaudible.

At length, Reuben heard what Asher had heard: a faint, rhythmic splash – further out to sea, but how far, he couldn't judge. Oars. Another boat.

Gradually, the sound faded. Reuben relaxed a little, but nobody else moved. Then Asher's voice hissed in sudden alarm.

'They're coming back!'

And Reuben could hear the oars again, lapping steadily towards him.

'Bull, raise the grappler, damn you!'

Bull heaved on the chain, but the iron hooks had stuck fast under rocks on the sea floor and the boat lurched and dipped backwards, so that Reuben felt the swirl of seawater round his legs as it poured in over the stern.

'Cast the chain!' Asher's voice was more than a whisper now.

Bull threw the chain overboard, the oarsmen heaved, and Reuben almost followed the chain as the boat churned in a swift circle.

'Heave to!' The voice behind them was frighteningly close in the darkness. 'Heave to or we fire!'

'It's that Boatman Gibbs,' muttered Bull. 'He'll not have us.'

And the overloaded boat ploughed away towards the shore.

The report of the pistol when it came shook the limpid night air like a cannon. Bull's hand pushed Reuben roughly to the slopping floor of the boat but Reuben still heard the fizz as the ball hit the water close behind him.

Then a second shot, and Daniel seemed to jerk sharply, but Reuben wasn't sure in the confusion, as Bull whispered loudly: 'Hard to port! Daniel, pull, boy! Seaward. Now. Now!'

An oar blade struck bottom as the boat swung wildly. They were perilously close to running aground, so close that Reuben could hear the gurgle and surge of the rising tide among the rocks. But the closeness to disaster was also their salvation, because the sound of their oars was now masked by that of the busy, breaking wavelets. They crept westward, keeping as tight under the Cormorant Cliff as they dared, Bull clambering to the bows and craning forward to fend off rocks when he saw them in time.

There were no more pistol shots. And when they heard another shout, it was not an order to heave to, but an exclamation, followed by curses and the dull bump and scrape of wood on rock. Their pursuers had run in too close.

Bull chuckled. 'That'll slow 'em. We'll turn in at Black Tooth.'

There was muttering from Asher but he didn't argue. Bull groped his way round the bulk of Sun Rock, a long high elbow of chalk that stuck out from the main cliff and concealed the entrance to a narrow channel. At the end of the channel was a beach.

Reuben was relieved when the boat finally ran ashore on soft shingle, but he reached out anxiously to Daniel, who had collapsed across his oar. It wasn't like him to be exhausted.

'Daniel,' whispered Reuben. 'Are you shot?'

Daniel merely shook his head and stumbled stiffly from the boat after the others.

The glowing yellow eye of the spout lantern showed a narrow black gap in the angled strata of the cliff face; a sea cave that couldn't be seen from out in the bay. It was the shape of a missing tooth. Black Tooth. It was not one of Reuben's favourite places. Nor Asher's.

'We shouldn't've come in here,' he growled, as the others slumped on the narrow pebbled beach outside the cave.

'There was no choice,' replied Bull. 'We'd never have made the Head against the tide.'

'Then we should've sunk the tubs again. We're trapped if they find the channel.'

'I've customers I can't keep waiting,' said Bull. 'And they blue-coats *won't* find the channel. It's hard enough to see in daylight, let alone pitch dark.'

Asher grunted sceptically.

'P'raps they got local knowledge,' he said, beginning to prowl. 'They knew we was out there.'

Bull was becoming irritated. He shook his head firmly.

'They're fresh, they're keen, they made a boat patrol. 'Twas luck they came across us, nothing more.'

But Asher wasn't satisfied. 'Well, let's hope their "luck" don't get no better.'

And he stared down hard at Reuben. 'Eh, nipper? You're not sayin' much.'

'Why?' asked Bull sharply. 'What should he say?'

'Nothin', p'raps.' Asher shrugged. 'Though if it's luck we're speakin' of, we've had our share of bad these past two days. Where might that precious London boy you saved be, right now?' He prodded Reuben with his foot. 'Sharin' a glass with Lieutenant Cade, mebbe?'

'No!' Reuben's protest sounded far too loud on the secret beach.

'Quiet!' ordered Bull. He stood up. 'Our luck's not so bad: we're alive, we've got our cargo. We must get it away, that's all.'

'And how do we do that?' asked Asher. 'With the tide comin' in to drown us, and the blue-coats waitin' to shoot us?'

'I'll climb the cliff,' offered Reuben. He sprang to his feet. 'I'll climb with the rope, then send it down for the tubs.'

'Up from Black Tooth in the dark?' Asher's tone was contemptuous in its disbelief.

'He's the only one of us who could,' grunted Bull, though he too was concerned. 'You sure, nipper?'

'Then you can get Daniel home,' said Reuben.

'Daniel?'

Bull didn't understand. He shone the spout lantern briefly to where Daniel was still sitting, head down. It illuminated a dark stain on his torn shirt. Bull crouched swiftly beside him and, ignoring Daniel's protest, lifted the shirt to reveal an ugly gash across the side of his chest.

Bull blew out his breath but said nothing to Daniel. He straightened up and turned to Reuben.

'I'll get the rope,' he muttered grimly.

The dragon's jaws bit into Reuben's shoulders as he climbed, and the long pole rapped the backs of his legs, trying to unbalance him.

The rope had been tied to the dragon's neck, and it trailed and dangled behind Reuben like an ever-lengthening tail. He couldn't see the cliff he

62

was climbing, but he moved as quickly as he dared, for when he *could* see the cliff, it would be too late: he too would be visible in the early summer dawn. Then, his impulsive offer to get the tubs off the beach would end in disaster.

It might well end in disaster anyway. To descend from a clifftop on a spiked rope in daylight was dangerous. To ascend this cliff blind, with only your fingers and toes for support, was little short of madness. Reuben had only his determination and his concern for Daniel to sustain him as he inched upwards. And his knowledge of the Cormorant Cliff. He knew it was formed of different layers of ancient rock, close together and straight, like the pages of a giant book, tilted diagonally. Pressing himself flat, he could edge sideways and upwards along its narrow ledges. The only trouble was he would be moving ever further away from Black Tooth, and would have to judge how far to return along the clifftop. If he reached it.

He was thinking he must be about two thirds of the way up, when the rising ledge he was feeling his way along became a sudden chasm ahead of him, a vertical drop created by a recent rockfall.

For more than a minute, Reuben stood quite still against the cliff, unable to move, trying to think. To retrace his cautious steps meant failure. To continue was impossible. Directly upwards was the only way. He reached for a fingerhold and, as he did so, a small shower of stones and dust bounced and fell on him from above. He paused, his heart thumping, but he knew he had to try. He reached again with both hands, and pulled himself up. A lump of cliff began to come away in his left hand but as he cried out softly in terror, someone snatched his wrist and clung on to it while he scrabbled desperately for a toehold and finally found one which took some of his weight. His other wrist was also grabbed now and, with this help, Reuben dragged himself up on to the wider ledge above.

He couldn't see who had saved him but he recognized the voice when Pin spoke.

'The top's quite close.'

He'd let go of Reuben's wrists, but Reuben reached out shakily and squeezed Pin's hand.

'Thank you,' he said. It wasn't enough by any means but it was all he had breath for.

'What's that on your back?' asked Pin.

'A dragon,' said Reuben. And he remembered why he was climbing the cliff.

The turf on the down above Black Tooth was lined with the deep wide cracks that Reuben was always wary of: splits in the ground near the cliff edge that one day would be the beginnings of rockfalls. Tonight, though, they must be his friend. Reuben tested the edge of one and, judging it firm enough, opened the dragon's jaws wide and plunged the curved hooks into the chalky soil. He tugged hard on the pole. The hooks stuck fast, even when tested with his full weight and Pin's added too.

Satisfied, Reuben made his way to the cliff edge, straightening the trailing rope as he went. He paused, listening to the incoming tide on the pebbles of the tiny beach far below, reassuring himself that he was, indeed, directly above Black Tooth. Then he lifted the rope high and let it drop. Slowly, deliberately, once, twice, three times. After the third lift and drop, an answering tug came from below. Then suddenly, the rope went taut and Reuben knew the first pair of tubs had been attached. Excited now, he called Pin to come and help, and the two of them braced themselves as best they could and hauled on the rope.

They could feel the tubs bumping against the cliff face as they ascended and Reuben feared they might snag, but at last they appeared in their sling, smooth, damp and gritted with chalk dust. Reuben was alarmed then that he could see the tubs so clearly.

'Quickly, Pin, now we must hide 'em!'

They dragged their load across the grass, untied the rope sling and pushed the tubs into the great crack in the earth. Still four more loads before daybreak. Reuben hurried back to the cliff edge and cast the rope into the greying darkness.

'You're mad.'

'And you're a misery. If you won't help, go to the boat and tend Daniel.'

Bull turned away from Asher and knotted the next pair of tubs to the dangling rope.

He was determined but it was going to be close. The eastern sky was glowing more yellow by the minute, and the incoming tide lapped his heels.

The tubs twirled and banged swiftly away above Bull's head. He wondered that Reuben had the strength to pull them up so fast on his own and warmed further to him. He was forgiven for saving the boy from the wreck. Reuben had saved Bull's bacon tonight.

Bull remembered the spout lantern and tied it quickly to the last pair of tubs. A wave soaked his back, Asher shouted at him from the boat to hurry, and Bull laughed out loud, defying those who would oppress him and, in particular, the over-mighty Boatman Gibbs.

Lieutenant Cade heard human voices. Or did he? Perhaps it was just the confounded seabirds.

The coastguard boat rocked in the growing swell and the oars creaked in their locks. Small waves chattered and slurped among the kelp.

The heightened stillness of the night had gone, but Lieutenant Cade was loath to finish the patrol. His men were tired and hungry but still alert. Sharp, as men lucky to have been chosen for employment should be. They were keen to impress. That wouldn't last, of course: they were only seamen, after all. Redundant seamen in a new force with a new uniform and the promise of decent wages and rewards. In all probability, officialdom wouldn't keep that promise, so Lieutenant Cade reckoned he had three months at most before slackness and discontent set in. Boatman Gibbs was different. Boatman Gibbs clearly shared his leader's zeal. A little too much, perhaps. But only success would keep the remainder brave and interested. And honest.

'Pull ahead, boys, if you please.'

Six oars cut the water as one, and the boat glided sleekly forward. Lieutenant Cade was pleased with the craft. Most of his work would be done on land, but he was confident that on the water he would have the catching of any so-called fishing boat. Darkness and a lifetime's familiarity with the coast had saved his quarry last night. It wouldn't happen again. He scanned the dawn-washed base of the rocky cliffs, noting every detail. If he had raised his eyes to their grassy tops, he might have seen two small boys scurrying upwards with a rope and disappearing into the ground like rabbits.

*

Reuben lay quite still. Things had gone wrong. Seconds earlier, he and Pin had been at the cliff edge, heaving up the last pair of tubs. But Bull, in his haste, couldn't have secured them properly, and as they'd been tugged up on to the grass, the knot had slipped and the tubs, still in their sling, had plummeted back to the beach below. Reuben had managed to grab the spout lantern, but as he stared after the tubs in helpless dismay, he'd seen the blue-coats.

Bull was in the boat as the tubs hit the beach and exploded, their staves springing open and the brandy inside disappearing in a brief gush. He hesitated. They shouldn't leave the tubs, shattered or otherwise. Then, as he made up his mind to leap from the boat and wade back ashore, a wave swept the length of the tiny beach and carried the debris away; and Bull grinned instead. Even the sea was on his side today. But as the boat left the channel and emerged from behind the shielding bulk of Sun Rock, Asher spoke.

'Company,' he said, making even this simple observation sound like a sneer.

Bull turned to see the coastguard boat bearing down on them. There was no hope of fleeing.

No need of it either, thought Bull calmly. No evidence remained on the boat. No tubs, no dragon, no grappler and chain, no spout lantern, not even a rope. And Daniel looked a little better in daylight.

He was hunched with his arm hiding the bloodstain on his shirt, and managed to ship his oar tidily as the coastguard boat pulled alongside.

'Good morning.' Lieutenant Cade politely raised his hat. 'Your business, if you please?'

'Fishing,' replied Bull.

The blue-coats had manoeuvred close and grabbed the gunwale of the boat, rafting their own craft up against it.

Lieutenant Cade gazed quizzically inboard.

'You have no nets.'

'Pot fishing,' said Bull. 'Lobster and crab.'

'You have no pots, either.'

'On our way to lift them now.' Bull pointed out into the bay, where a series of faded scraps of cloth fluttered on spindly sticks above the water. 'Those are our marks.'

'You have no meat to re-bait your pots.' Lieutenant Cade smiled at Bull.

Bull smiled back. 'A cormorant stole it.'

Lieutenant Cade nodded towards Sun Rock and the channel behind it.

'And this is your home port?' Let the smirking rogue talk his way out of that.

'No,' said Bull, unconcerned. 'Our home port is the cottages. We lost some pots in the storm and have been searchin' for 'em.'

'You should have asked our assistance,' piped up Boatman Gibbs.

'We're good at searching.'

It was a taunt, pricking the memory of the humiliating raid on the cottages and boats two nights ago, but Bull paused long enough to control his temper. He nodded slowly.

'Good at searching, yes,' he acknowledged. 'But not at finding.' And he smiled again.

The gunwales of the boats knocked and rubbed against each other in the swell, forehead to forehead, like posturing prizefighters. It was a beautiful morning. The sun had risen now.

'Cast off,' ordered Lieutenant Cade suddenly. He seemed no longer interested in the fishermen.

Boatman Gibbs was locked in a mutual stare of dislike with Bull, and continued staring as he pushed the boat away, hard, and took up his oar. Bull spat elegantly into the widening gap of water between them.

'To starboard, if you please,' continued Lieutenant Cade, ignoring Bull's provocation.

'I'll do more than spit at you,' said Gibbs coldly, still holding the look as he rowed away.

Lieutenant Cade's attention was on the channel beyond the great rock, and Bull and his crew could only sit and watch as the coastguard boat rounded the rock and disappeared.

Bull shrugged. 'There's nothin' for 'em there,' he reassured the others.

'Unless nipper returns on his rope,' grunted Asher.

'He's not stupid,' said Daniel, but his voice was weak and so were his arms now. Bull quickly shifted him to the bows and took his place at the oar.

Reuben did as he'd been told. Having tucked the tubs as deeply in the fissure as they could, and covered them loosely with clods of turf torn from other crevices and scrapes in the downland grass, he and Pin headed northwards over the shoulder of the down, away from Cormorant Bay. They took the dragon with them, together with the rope and spout lantern. These they hid in the shepherd's hut, as directed, before turning towards home.

Despite his relief and gratitude, a niggling doubt had begun to gnaw at Reuben.

'Why was you on the cliff?' he asked.

'Why shouldn't I be?' retorted Pin, sensing suspicion.

'Asher says the blue-coats was out there cos you squealed on us,' said Reuben.

'What?' cried Pin. 'Well, p'raps I should've done, if that's what *you* think.' He sounded really angry.

'I never said it's what I think.'

'I followed you cos you made so much noise leavin',' said Pin scornfully. 'Then I saw a lantern. *Twice.* You deserve to get caught. And I'm better on a cliff than you are.'

Reuben didn't argue. 'I'm sorry,' he said.

'Good, cos I never squealed in me life.'

They walked in uncomfortable silence for a while.

'Take me with you next time,' said Pin. 'I'd be useful.'

Reuben wasn't sure he wanted there to be a next time. The sinister reality of the exciting rendezvous had been his brother getting shot.

'What's that?' asked Pin abruptly, his righteous indignation undermined by what he'd heard.

'What?'

'That noise. Sounds like babies crying.'

Reuben listened, then slowly realized what Pin meant.

'It is,' he said sadly. 'Mothers that can't afford to keep 'em leave 'em out on the downs here.'

He glanced at Pin and took pleasure in the appalled stare he got in return. It was a guilty pleasure, but he couldn't let the know-all London boy have things all his own way.

Waves rolled into the cave's throat then foamed back again, as if Black Tooth were spewing them out. Lieutenant Cade felt a breath of cold clammy air envelop him as the swell lifted the boat in through the mouth of the cave. The oar blades touched the sides and if there was a secret beach at the inward end when the tide was low, there was none now. The cave was only three or four boats long and already the insurging waves were sprawling up the end wall. No beach. And no contraband.

'Out again, sir?'

The roof of the cave was white, sea-smoothed and close. Boatman Gibbs didn't want to be still inside when a wave filled it.

Lieutenant Cade nodded. 'Out again.'

He ducked his head as the boat re-emerged into the warm daylight, and scanned the cliffs above. Samphire and seabirds, nothing else. Then something caught his eye in the rocks not yet fully submerged at the eastern end of the channel.

At first, Lieutenant Cade thought he'd seen a corpse, for the cave and the channel were the sort of places where drowned sailors from the recent wreck might well have been carried by the current and tide. But as he drew closer and reached for the boathook, he saw that he'd found something far more useful than a dead body. He'd found a rope sling, and a clutch of splintered barrel staves.

5

Treason

A familiar crowd had gathered on the beach when Reuben and Pin arrived home: fishermen and villagers who'd heard the gunfire in the night and come to satisfy their curiosity.

Asher was lounging against Daniel's drawn-up boat but Bull was pacing outside the Hibberds' cottage. Inside, Molly was cleaning and binding her husband's damaged ribs with Grampy's help. Daniel hadn't previously told her the true purpose of his night fishing, and she'd included Bull in her condemnation, which had been uncharacteristically fierce when she'd found out. She'd used words she could have learnt only from Dinah.

Bull cheered up on seeing Reuben, though he frowned again when the London boy appeared behind him.

'Well done, nipper!' he cried, clapping Reuben on the shoulder. 'Is the crop well planted?'

'As well as can be,' said Reuben, 'but two fell.'

'Not your fault,' said Bull dismissively. 'Where's *he* been?' He was eyeing Pin with caution.

'On the cliff,' said Reuben. 'He helped me. He's a good climber,' he added, feeling generosity was in order.

'Is he now?' Bull nodded warily but then the frown returned as he heard approaching horses and turned to see blue-coats arriving above the ladder.

'Now what they after?' he growled.

Lieutenant Cade left his horse with the others this time but descended the ladder as nimbly as his men. He carried a canvas bag. Reuben saw that Boatman Gibbs was carrying an axe.

Lieutenant Cade approached Bull and Asher, though his gaze took in the others present.

'You've been playing games with us, gentlemen,' he said. 'But I can assure you there will be only one winner.'

He emptied the contents of the canvas bag at Bull's feet. Bull saw barrel staves and knotted rope but didn't blink.

'Found at the hidden beach with the sea cave, shortly after you left it this morning.' Lieutenant Cade picked up two of the barrel staves and the rope and held them in front of Bull.

'These staves are undoubtedly French, as any wine merchant will testify. And this rope, as a man of your seafaring knowledge will recognize, is laid the opposite way to normal rope: to prevent it unravelling when used to carry tubs.'

Out of the corner of his eye, Bull saw Daniel emerge from his cottage. He wore a heavy tunic in place of his torn and bloodied shirt.

'And what's this to do with us?' asked Bull of Lieutenant Cade. 'We're not responsible for every piece of flotsam washed ashore.' He nodded at the evidence and shrugged. 'If it's from France, go and bully the French.'

'Don't seek to make a fool of me!'

Lieutenant Cade almost lost his temper. That wouldn't do. The evidence was circumstantial. He knew that as well as the smirking, disrespectful tide-waders. It was frustrating, but discipline was everything.

'You know how close to the wind you're sailing, Oliver,' he said quietly. 'I shall have you red-handed very soon.'

'Yes, teacher,' replied Bull, and the small crowd laughed, whereupon Boatman Gibbs swung his axe at Daniel's boat and hacked a chunk of timber from its bows.

The crowd erupted, rushing forward, and Lieutenant Cade himself pushed Gibbs away.

'It's the law, sir,' Gibbs protested cynically. 'A smuggler's boat must be sawn in three.'

He preferred an axe to a saw, himself: it was more warlike. But in the uproar, he didn't see

Daniel come at him until the axe was being twisted furiously from his grasp.

'Touch my boat once more and you are dead!' snarled Daniel, brandishing the axe in Gibbs's face.

But Bull snatched the axe from him and hurled it far into the sea, as Molly came running from the cottage.

'Daniel, stop, stop!' she pleaded and, with Bull's muscular help, she wrestled her husband clear, though Daniel's tongue was not to be restrained.

'I wish to God the French had won at Waterloo!' he shouted wildly. 'We could fare no worse than this!'

He was almost laughing in his fury and despair but allowed Molly and Reuben to lead him backwards towards the cottage. Molly could feel warm blood seeping through the tight bandage beneath his tunic. Suddenly, he collapsed and fell but recovered enough to sit upright on the beach and cry out again passionately.

'Where's liberty and justice? Not in England!'

'Search them, and search the boat,' ordered Lieutenant Cade tersely. 'And take care!' The zeal of Boatman Gibbs, he'd decided, was a liability.

Two blue-coats grabbed Bull and roughly felt inside his shirt and pockets. There were other kinds of contraband besides tubs of brandy: lace and tea could be easily concealed about the person. Bull submitted to the manhandling with dumb insolence. So did Asher, having been seized as he moved swiftly from the boat. Then the blue-coats turned towards Daniel, the third man out on the bay that morning, and Molly felt a fresh surge of alarm.

'Sir! I have something!'

Boatman Gibbs called in sudden triumph and all eyes turned from Daniel to his boat.

Gibbs was stooped, delving in the small stern locker. When he turned, he was holding up a wax-sealed packet.

There was a moment of surprised silence. No one, blue-coat, fisherman or villager had expected such a find or knew what it might imply.

Lieutenant Cade strode towards Gibbs and took the packet. He turned it over, examining it carefully, then looked to Daniel, who still sat where he'd half fallen on the pebbles.

'Can you write, Master Hibberd?' asked Lieutenant Cade.

'A little.' Daniel nodded vaguely. He was feeling faint.

'And who do you know in Cherbourg that you should take a letter to?'

Bull glanced quizzically across at Daniel. He himself knew someone in Cherbourg, or from Cherbourg. Was Daniel doing business with him too? Surely not. And by letter? They were dangerous things, letters. Bull was glad he couldn't write.

'Cherbourg?' echoed Daniel, as Lieutenant Cade walked slowly towards him.

Lieutenant Cade nodded and read aloud the address on the packet.

'To January. Of the League of Bold and Ardent Hopes. Cherbourg.'

Bull relaxed a little. The man he knew from Cherbourg was called Philippe.

Daniel was looking up blankly. Lieutenant Cade showed him the packet. Daniel shook his head.

'That's not my hand.'

Lieutenant Cade hesitated then broke the seal on the packet, removed the string and unfolded the thick paper on which Reuben, edging closer, could see a letter written. Lieutenant Cade scanned the contents before speaking again.

'You write fluently for a fisherman,' he said quietly.

'That is not my hand,' repeated Daniel.

'And have a fervent desire for revolution, it would seem,' continued Lieutenant Cade.

He stared down at Daniel, who stared back, trying to find his voice.

'Revolution?'

'Shall I read this to you?' asked Lieutenant Cade more strongly, then shook his head and turned away. 'Let me read it to your friends instead. Though perhaps they already know its contents and approve.' He paused, regarded his audience, then read aloud:

> '*Our plans progress apace. The Throne of Justice awaits its True Sovereign. That is: the People.*
>
> *The Bold and Ardent Hopes of France, of Italy, of Spain, of Greece, shall not find England wanting when the moment comes. King George will fall as surely as will every Tyrant and his court in Europe.*
>
> *Send word when your friends will come. The Poor of our country are hungry for their Words and Weapons.*
>
> *Your Eager Disciple in the Cause,*
> *September.'*

There was a murmur in the crowd. Lieutenant Cade turned to Daniel, his shock and disgust evident.

'These words are treason, Master Hibberd. And you know the penalty for that.'

'I did not write the letter!' Daniel struggled to his feet, pain and faintness forgotten in his bewilderment and sudden fear. Molly clutched his arm.

'It was in your boat,' declared Lieutenant Cade. 'You go to sea. To France, or to Frenchies in the Channel. You are condemned out of your own mouth: you state you wish the French had won at Waterloo.'

'I meant no treason!' cried Daniel. 'Only that it would make no difference to our condition if they had!'

'This letter seeks to put that theory to the test,' said Lieutenant Cade.

Someone tugged at his arm and he turned sharply. A boy was standing there. Not the urchin he'd shrugged away from his horse two days ago. Much taller. Lieutenant Cade recognized him from the cottage raid. Another Hibberd. He was holding a Bible, as threadbare as his clothes.

'Will you look inside, please, sir?'

The boy's hands were trembling but his eyes were steady.

'Do you wish for a sermon, then?' asked the officer brusquely.

Reuben shook his head. 'Read the writing, sir. Please.'

Lieutenant Cade took the Bible and opened it. The flyleaf was damp and discoloured but the blotched writing on it was clear enough:

This Bible given to me by my father Joseph Hibberd 10th July 1816. Daniel Hibberd.

The handwriting was ill-formed and painstaking, nothing like the flowing hand of the letter.

Lieutenant Cade stared at the inscription a long time, deciding what to do. Daniel Hibberd had not written the letter, that was patently clear. But it was in his boat; that made him a courier, if nothing else. And he must know who *had* written it. That was still treason.

The boy tugged his arm again, as if he'd guessed what Lieutenant Cade was thinking.

'Sir, anyone could've put that letter in our boat. Even Boatman Gibbs.'

Lieutenant Cade looked up slowly. The boy still didn't flinch from his gaze. There was no insolence or accusation in his voice. It was a simple statement of fact. For the briefest moment, Lieutenant Cade imagined Boatman Gibbs might not be above such an outrage, but when he dismissed the thought, so many other possibilities occurred to him that for once he was at a loss. At the very least, he supposed, he should arrest Hibberd and pass him on for questioning. But Lieutenant Cade was an exact man as well as a patriot. He disliked acting on supposition. He closed the Bible and gave it back to the boy, then folded the letter methodically and put it in his pocket.

'Do not give me cause to regret this,' he said to Daniel, then walked away.

Boatman Gibbs looked incredulous. At length, he shook his head and laughed.

'You owe me an axe,' he whispered in Bull's ear as he passed.

'You may have it in your skull at any time,' replied Bull.

The blue-coats followed Lieutenant Cade back to the ladder, Boatman Gibbs still shaking his head.

Having mounted his horse, Lieutenant Cade turned to his men. He didn't feel the need to explain his actions but the letter clearly gave a new dimension to their duties. He took it from his pocket.

'It would seem there are spies and plotters on this coast as well as smugglers,' he said. 'Be vigilant.'

He'd realized by now that of course the letter could have been written far from the coast. In London, or Manchester. Anywhere. That was the way of revolutionaries: to keep themselves well hidden and construct networks of communication that spread underground like a fungus. But if the rogues here in Cormorant Bay were the outlet, he would show no more mercy. One proof was all he required. Just one.

'There will be a reward for the coastguard who leads me to the writer of this letter. Or to his willing accomplice. A generous reward.'

He hoped the boy who'd brought the Bible was not involved.

No one left on the beach moved or spoke until the blue-coats had ridden away. Then everyone talked at once, and Daniel sat down shakily again.

Pin had stayed in the background when he'd seen the blue-coats. Now, he came forward as Reuben went to put the Bible back indoors.

'What was that they found?'

'A letter,' said Reuben. 'Someone wants to turn out King George.'

'What, cut off his head like the Frenchies did to theirs?'

Pin seemed more excited than upset by the idea. Reuben had heard of the French Revolution. It had happened long before he was born. And he knew there'd been a war in Europe and at sea because of it. That was when Grampy had lost his foot. But he didn't really understand.

'Who'd we have as king instead?' he wondered.

'Not Boatman Gibbs, I hope,' said Pin.

While speculation bubbled around him, Bull was going through in his mind the names of those he knew who could write properly. There weren't many and they were all rich, and since, as he'd once heard it said, it was difficult to agitate on a full stomach, they seemed unlikely plotters of revolution. Squire Coleman was only interested in hunting. Mr Pocock spent all his time on his collection of stuffed birds. Parson Teague, who was charitable in such a cold, dry way? Bull didn't like Parson Teague. He could imagine him having a secret Cause, writing a letter with many capital letters in it.

He squatted beside Daniel and spoke secretively.

'Not from the parson, is it?'

'What?'

Daniel was looking pale and flushed at one and the same time.

'Your bit of private work.'

'For pity's sake, Bull, I know nothing of that letter!'

Bull took no notice but leant closer.

'Only when Cade mentioned Cherbourg of all places . . . well, you do know there's somethin' in the offing, don't you? Our biggest yet. I wouldn't want no complications.'

'Complications? I think we have enough, Bull.'

Daniel laughed then winced, and slid sideways into Molly's lap.

That night, his wound was worse: hot and weeping, and the fever that came with it rising.

Molly was a good and capable nurse, and so was Grampy, but they had only salt water with which to treat the torn flesh. This would have been enough if the wound was simple. Grampy, though, had seen many gunshot wounds and now worried in case a scrap of lead from the shot was hidden inside, lodged against a rib. They had no means of knowing without cutting Daniel open, and little money for a doctor with the skill and knowledge needed. Besides, there was no doctor in the village, and if one was willing to come at all from town, he would recognize the cause of the injury and be suspicious. Then report his suspicions to the coastguards.

Bull Oliver called in briefly to see how Daniel was, then slipped away. There was unfinished business, but no point in stirring Molly up again by mentioning it. He nodded once at Reuben as he went and Reuben understood.

It was hard to hear the church clock when the wind was wrong, but Reuben was ready when it struck one.

He hadn't slept much anyway, taking a turn to sit with Daniel while Grampy dozed and Molly fed Francis. They were both awake now, Molly bathing Daniel's forehead with a scrap of wet cloth; Grampy just sitting. Reuben crept out behind them and through the back door.

He went to the shelter and found the London boy curled among the lobster pots.

'Pin,' whispered Reuben. 'Wake up.'

He shook Pin's arm and Pin sat bolt upright, toppling a lobster pot noisily in his alarm.

'Sshh . . . You said I should take you with me next time. This is it.'

Pin didn't speak but after a second he scrambled up and they slipped away together, climbed the ladder and headed quickly west towards the Cormorant Cliff, its chalky flank palely visible in the starlight.

'It's dangerous,' said Reuben quietly, when they were well clear of the cottages. 'Transportation to the colonies if we're caught. Or hanging.'

'Doesn't frighten me, I've been close to both before now,' said Pin, not boasting, just secretly excited to be involved. Trusted. 'I stowed away on the *Calicut* cos I was a wanted man.'

'Wanted? You mean there was a price on you?'

Reuben had never met a real criminal. Smugglers didn't count. He remembered his suspicions when Pin had lied at breakfast. His dark thoughts seemed mean-minded now: Pin had proved his courage and his worth.

'Not a price, exactly,' Pin admitted with reluctance. A five-hundred-pound lie was difficult to resist but they were being honest with each other. 'Just, the Charlies, the constables, the runners, they know your face. You get taken for what you didn't do as well as what you did. Pick up a crust in London and they swear you stole it.' He was aware this might sound self-pitying, so he said bluntly, 'I have stole lead from rooves. And ladies' gloves from a shop. You can peach on me if you like, if I let you down.'

'You won't,' said Reuben.

Bull seemed less sure when they met at the shepherd's hut. He still scowled mistrustfully at Pin.

'We need him now we've not got Daniel,' urged Reuben. 'I'll vouch for him.'

'We'll hold you to that,' said Asher unpleasantly.

But Bull was anxious to be moving and he quickly put aside his misgivings. 'Show us where the tubs are, nipper.'

Reuben and Pin led the way up over the down. Pin could hear the babies again but was too unnerved by them to mention it. Apart from Bull and Asher, there were two other men with them. Reuben whispered that their names were Noyce and Cotton. These two said nothing, but Asher muttered critically all the way; especially when they reached the clifftop and Reuben darted back and forth anxiously for some time, trying to locate the tubs. There were many deep cracks in the turf and they all looked much the same in darkness. And Bull insisted they be sparing with the spout lantern.

'Here!' called Pin softly, at last, and he'd pulled aside most of the loose turves by the time the others reached him.

Bull shone the lantern briefly. The tubs were all there, though hard to see in the gloom, but Pin noticed something different about one of them: a white cross scrawled on the tub's side. The others saw it too.

'Who saw you plantin' these?' Bull's voice was sharp.

'No one,' said Reuben, though he felt less certain than he sounded.

'Well, someone's marked 'em.'

'Gums?' ventured Reuben. 'Should we leave one?'

'We've lost two already,' said Bull, irritated. 'I'll not give up another to a meddling old shepherd.'

He quietly began lifting out the pairs of tubs, handing them to Asher and the other men. Pin wanted to ask about the cross but got no chance.

'You and the boy are takin' Daniel's part in this then, are you?' Bull sounded dubious again.

'Just give us our load and we'll be gone,' said Reuben eagerly.

He sensed Bull hesitate in the darkness, then a pair of tubs was dumped at his feet.

'Braidstone,' said Bull briskly. 'You know your way?'

'I do.'

'Starling Cottage, bottom of the lane. Miss it and you'll end in the river. Mother Cowley's the name. She owes you five shillun. Don't come back without it.'

Bull slung the last pair of tubs over his own shoulder.

'Good luck, nippers,' he said. 'Home by dawn, mind. No dawdling.' He paused. 'And don't get taken.'

He hurried away and Reuben realized the

others had already gone. Only he and Pin remained. Now he began to feel nervous, because he hadn't admitted to Bull what he was planning. Nor to Pin.

'Can you carry both tubs on your own?' he asked.

The rope chafed Pin's shoulders, even through the sacking cape that Reuben had found for him in the shepherd's hut. And the tubs, still attached to the sling as they had been when hooked from the seabed, seemed heavier now than when he and Reuben had hauled them up the cliff. Much heavier. Pin tottered along the starlit lane with one tub bouncing against his chest and the other bumping on his back, their contents glugging rhythmically as he walked. It was painful work but Pin was determined to succeed, even if the rope harness cut his shoulders to the bone. And not just for the share of the five shillings he'd been promised.

He'd parted from Reuben some minutes ago. Reuben was going to a town called Alvershill. With a gun.

Reuben wasn't sure now that he should have trusted Pin so entirely. He'd shown him the Nest. He'd shown him the rifles. But since Pin was now risking at least his liberty by delivering the tubs, it had been the right thing to do. Besides, if Reuben ran into trouble in Alvershill, it would be useful that someone knew where he'd gone.

He'd taken one rifle from the crate and wrapped it in a sack. He knew there was a man in the town who bought such things. Anything, in fact. With Daniel out of action, Reuben felt keenly the sudden responsibility as head of the family. The sole breadwinner. He must take every opportunity to earn money, and it had occurred to him that he might get more for a rifle than for delivering a tub. He should be back home at much the same time. With every step he took towards Alvershill, though, he became more anxious about Pin. He'd explained the route carefully, but the way to Braidstone wasn't easy. Especially for a London boy in the dark.

Pin himself had no anxieties when he and Reuben first separated. The landmarks he'd been told to watch for loomed reassuringly in the correct order: the farmhouse with the lopsided chimney, the crossroads, the pond and reed bed. But then the sky dragged a blanket of cloud over itself and the starlight went out, and Pin became at first annoyed that smuggling must be always conducted in pitch blackness, and then concerned that he was lost because the lane he was following had narrowed to a grassy downhill path.

The next landmark was to be a windmill, which seemed unlikely to be on low ground, and Pin was about to retrace his steps when he heard hoof beats: a single horse, walking unhurriedly down the path behind him.

It was impossible to run away under the weight of the tubs, and the hedges on either side of the path had become suddenly high and impenetrable, with vicious thorns. Pin backed as far into the hedge as he could but was still only a pace from the path as the horse approached. It seemed impossible that the rider should neither see nor hear him and Pin was on the point of blurting out some kind of innocent greeting when the man on the horse dug in his heels and urged the horse into a canter. Pin smelt the horse and felt the thump of its hooves on the ground as it passed by, but no one challenged him. He remained quite still until absolute silence had been restored, then blundered on, forgetting to turn back in search of the windmill.

Eventually, the grassy path petered out in a low-lying marsh, and although Pin skirted the increasingly boggy ground as best he could, it soon cunningly surrounded him, so that every careful step on to firm turf ended in a struggle to pull his feet from cold, sucking mud. Then the temptation to heave off his burden of tubs and leave them to sink, while he himself made off and never returned to Cormorant Bay, became almost irresistible. For a few moments, the fact that Reuben trusted him ceased to matter. Indeed, Pin feared he might have said too much about his own past, and that he wasn't trusted at all, and had been deliberately sent astray to lose himself here. But that was stupid. Why would Reuben have wasted two precious tubs on him? He floundered on and gradually was rewarded by firmer ground and then a low hill with trees on it, and excitedly he recognized a great oak with three trunks, like a giant candelabrum. Another landmark.

Soon, Pin was striding down a broad lane into the hamlet of Braidstone. He found Starling Cottage, low and thatched, with a broken gate, and eased his way round to the overgrown back door. His quiet knock was answered by a sharp, wary voice. A woman's voice. Mother Cowley.

'Who's there?'

'Catch from Cormorant Bay,' replied Pin, as Reuben had instructed him.

He heard what he thought was a bolt being drawn but then realized that a small hatch had opened at head height in the door. He was being scrutinized.

'I was told two o'clock,' grumbled the woman inside, but she turned a heavy key, drew more bolts and rattled the door open.

Pin stepped indoors and found himself in a long

low-ceilinged room, lit by a large smoking candle and the glow of a fire in a wide hearth at the far end. The room smelt of a pungent mix of raw brandy and something burnt and sweet. Mother Cowley hurried to the hearth and scraped and banged violently with a ladle at the contents of a large soot-covered cooking pot.

'I've burnt the sugar black cos of you,' she snapped. 'Put 'em on the table, then.'

Pin had barely lifted the tubs from his aching shoulders before she'd knocked them open with a hammer and chisel and started pouring the contents into the cooking pot.

'Water, quickly!' she ordered, then, 'Slowly! Don't drown it!' as Pin emptied the bucket she'd nodded at into the pot.

The hot intoxicating fumes filled his head so that he thought he would faint but Mother Cowley impatiently pushed him away and thrust five shilling pieces into his hand, before bustling to a cupboard from which she started taking empty glass bottles.

Pin hesitated then turned to the door.

'Well, tidy up before you go!' cried Mother Cowley.

Pin was at a loss and just looked helpless as she came back to the table with a clutch of bottles.

'Rope and barrel on the fire, boy. Ain't you had no education at all? Dear oh me.'

She picked up the rope sling and dangled it ominously, like a noose.

'What's burnt can't hang you,' she said, and tossed the sling into the hearth.

The rope was damp and smouldered acridly before flaring up, by which time she'd broken up the barrels with her hammer and begun to feed them to the fire too.

'Can you find your way home?' she asked, turning. 'I'm not sure you're up to this game.'

'Course I can,' said Pin.

And when Mother Cowley had hustled him out again and bolted the door behind him, he felt confident and happy. His errand was accomplished and the five shillings were safe in his pocket.

Another dangerous dawn was beginning to break as Pin retraced his steps up the lane, but a mist curling from the nearby marshes gave him a sense of being hidden. Not that there was anyone about to hide from now. Nevertheless, when he realized he still had the rough sacking cape round his shoulders, he hurriedly pulled it off and threw it in the ditch, feeling that it marked him as a tub-runner.

The lane opened on to a broad hillside and above the mist Pin glimpsed the landmark windmill far ahead. He was on his way. Then he heard the sound he'd come to dread above all others. First distant, then closer, then all around him. He was surrounded by the invisible babies. Their cries were pitiful, yet somehow sinister. They spoke of abandonment and hurt and despair; of utter desolation. Pin couldn't bear to listen, but couldn't move. He sank to his haunches, helpless with fear and sudden exhaustion, and squatted with his arms over his head in an attempt to shut out the inhumanity around him.

Then, in a merciful interlude of silence, he heard a new sound. A peculiar tugging, rasping noise just a couple of paces away. It moved remorselessly closer, then something barged against him and Pin opened his eyes, and even in the murk he recognized the bulk and smell of a sheep.

It bleated, apparently at Pin, but instantly the piteous cry of an invisible baby answered; then another and another, as newborn offspring all over the field called for their mothers' milk. Pin had been petrified by lambs. He began to sob, then laugh. He remembered word for word how Reuben had tricked him with his story of human mothers too poor to feed their infants, and stopped laughing. Anger welled up inside, anger and hurt pride. Then he saw the funny side and laughed again, louder still. But he promised himself that when he paid Reuben his five shillings for the tubs, he'd pay him with a punch on the nose too.

Pin jumped up, ready to run all the way back

to Cormorant Bay, only to find a horse standing in front of him amid the sheep. Steam was rising from its flanks, like the mist from the grass, and Boatman Gibbs was sitting on its back. Smiling.

6

Interrogation

'What is your name?'

'Pin, sir.'

He had decided to be polite and truthful where he could and say nothing where he could not.

Lieutenant Cade looked steadily at him from the other side of the table.

'Is that your real name?'

'It's the only one I have, sir.'

He could hear the echo of his own voice in the bare room. Lieutenant Cade's pen scratched loudly, and when he moved his chair on the stone floor, the scrape set Pin's teeth on edge. He stared at the wall above Lieutenant Cade's head. The whitewash was barely dry and Pin could smell it. The whole coastguard station smelt new.

'Where did you deliver your tubs?'

'What tubs, sir?'

Lieutenant Cade picked up the piece of sacking and shook it out delicately across the table in front of him, as if laying a cloth for breakfast.

He pointed calmly at two indented lines in the hemp, where the rope sling had bitten into the fibres.

'The tubs carried in the rope that made these marks. Before you threw the sacking into the ditch.'

Pin said nothing.

'Take off your shirt,' said Lieutenant Cade, as he wrote again in his large, lined book. He looked up. 'Take off your shirt.'

Pin pulled the thin ragged garment over his head. He knew his collar bone and shoulder blades would be red raw. He was glad he'd disposed of the five shillings; dropped the coins quietly on the grass as he'd been brought to the coastguard station on Boatman Gibbs's horse. At least he couldn't be asked awkward questions about why he had money. He'd go back later and pick it up. Assuming he was released.

'Turn round.'

Pin faced the door. The pen scratched in the book behind him.

'Put on your shirt and look at me.'

Pin did as he was told. Lieutenant Cade continued writing as he spoke.

'I am writing down evidence, Pin. I am writing down what Boatman Gibbs has told me, and what I can see.'

He looked up. 'Do you know what I mean by evidence?'

Pin nodded. He was familiar with the term.

'What were you carrying to make those marks on you, if not tubs?'

Pin didn't answer.

'Who gave you your load, tubs or otherwise, to carry to Braidstone?'

Pin looked at the floor, and Lieutenant Cade sat back in his chair, considering him with a sad, quizzical smile.

'Where were you born, Pin?'

'London, sir.'

'So how do you come to be here?'

'The shipwreck, sir.'

Lieutenant Cade raised his eyebrows a little, then nodded.

'I see.'

He stood up and wandered to the small window, peering out as he spoke casually.

'And do you have family?'

'None, sir.'

'How old are you, Pin?'

'Twelve years, I believe, sir.'

Lieutenant Cade was still looking out of the window.

'Have you heard of such a thing as a house of correction?'

Pin didn't reply immediately.

'Pin?'

'Yes, sir. I have heard of them.'

'There is such a house in Alvershill, the largest town hereabouts.' Lieutenant Cade turned and smiled. 'We are not entirely lacking in the amenities of civilization, you see.'

He began to walk round the room with measured thoughtful steps, explaining patiently to Pin as he did so.

'There is a law, Pin, designed for the very proper purpose of suppressing smuggling, whereby if a person is found loitering within five miles of the sea coast, or any navigable river – and Braidstone is both – that person may be considered suspicious. And if so considered, he may be taken before a magistrate. And the magistrate, if the person brought before him is unable, or unwilling, to give a satisfactory account of himself, has the power to commit him to the house of correction.' He paused behind Pin. 'There to be whipped and kept at hard labour for an entire month. An entire month.' He moved on and sat down unhurriedly, before speaking again. 'I should take you before the magistrate with extreme reluctance, Pin. But your behaviour was suspicious. There is evidence. And you cannot or will not explain yourself.' He shrugged and gazed at Pin. 'Perhaps you can say what other path is open to me in the performance of my duty?'

Boatman Gibbs prowled the passage between Lieutenant Cade's office and the guardroom with growing irritation. His Chief Officer's reasonable, well-modulated voice was clearly audible. Why was he still talking to the boy? Why not simply beat a confession out of him? And then extract the names of his accomplices by similar means.

The war against France had ended too soon for Boatman Gibbs. He itched for the simple uncurbed freedom of battle, where you attacked your enemy with ferocity and without hesitation. In his view, law enforcement should be conducted in the same way. Smuggling would die out overnight if those suspected were simply beaten or shot.

The innocent would have nothing to fear from such an approach: Boatman Gibbs had been able to tell exactly who the smugglers were during that very first afternoon at Cormorant Bay. In any case, even those not actively involved in running cargo were complicit. The entire community was involved, if only in silent approval. There were no innocents.

Lieutenant Cade intended to impose his will on these people but he'd have more luck catching eels in a bottomless bucket. Better to shoot the lot and be done with it. That would put an end to all these revolutionary mutterings, as well. Dead men didn't talk treason.

*

'Sit down, Pin,' said Lieutenant Cade, 'you're looking shaky.'

Pin didn't want to sit down. Doing so would imply a kind of capitulation, a readiness to talk.

'Sit down.'

Pin obeyed but continued to look at the floor. Lieutenant Cade leant forward, chin resting on his folded knuckles.

'I'm prepared to believe you have been forced into working for these people.' He sounded almost kind. 'The sea has cast you up among them. You have no means of escape. You are in their power.' He shrugged. 'It is understandable. Excusable. But what *you* must understand, Pin, is that these people are not your true friends. They have used you and you owe them nothing.' He paused. 'Nor are they true friends of their country. Your country. How is it, do you think, that the wages of our army are paid? Or our navy. Do you think the brave men who defend our nation and keep us free live on thin air? Do you think that, Pin?'

Pin shook his head. His voice was quiet.

'No, sir.'

'Then you are wise,' said Lieutenant Cade sincerely. 'They are fed and clothed and armed by money raised in taxes. Does it not follow then, that every tub of brandy or bale of baccy brought secretly into this country and sold untaxed means less money for those who need it most? Is not someone who knowingly denies money to our defenders in that way a traitor? Are *you* a traitor, Pin?'

The sun was shining in Alvershill, and Reuben wished it wasn't. The man was examining the rifle. Now he thrust it back at him.

'Sorry, can't help you.'

'But why not?'

Reuben was dismayed, as much at the prospect of having to carry the gun back to Cormorant Bay in what was now broad daylight as by his failure to sell it. He'd waited outside half the night, only to be rejected in half a minute.

'Too singular,' said the man. 'New model. Not been fired. Army, is it?' He looked at Reuben and sniffed. 'Too risky for the likes of me. Sorry.'

He opened the door, then paused and peered at Reuben.

'You sell feathers, don't you?'

'On market day, yes, sir.'

'Should've brought me a bagful. I know a woman who makes hats. I'd've given you a shillun.'

Outside in the accusing glare of the sun, Reuben pulled off his shirt and wrapped it round the rifle barrel that protruded starkly from its sack, then slunk away from the waking town.

*

Pin was free, but he didn't feel free at all. Lieutenant Cade had confused him. It was not so much the veiled threat of whipping and hard labour, it was the fact that, although Pin had given no information, Lieutenant Cade had let him go. And required him to think. But did Pin really owe the smugglers nothing? By which, Lieutenant Cade meant loyalty. Had they simply used him? *Were* they traitors to their country? Or simply poor people like himself, surviving as best they could in harsh conditions and in the face of harsher laws. Was a tub of cheap brandy really going to be the downfall of England?

By the time Cormorant Bay came into view, Pin had decided it was not. And he did owe the beach people something. He owed Reuben five shillings, to start with. So he couldn't go straight home. He turned away from the sea and climbed through a thick hawthorn hedge, just in case Boatman Gibbs was following. As he ran off to find his money, he was surprised that Cormorant Bay and home were now the same thought.

Reuben slid the rifle back into the Nest with weary relief and emerged on to the track, bracing himself to explain his absence to Molly.

'Good morning, my boy.'

Reuben stopped guiltily. He was just a few paces from the elder trees and nettles. Mr Pocock was striding up the track towards him, carrying the notebook he always took on what he called his nature walks.

'A fine day,' said Mr Pocock cheerfully. 'Not bird-hunting?'

'Uh, no, sir,' mumbled Reuben. He didn't think Mr Pocock could have seen where he'd come from, because of the bend in the track, but he could feel himself blushing again. He wished he had Pin's confidence.

'Pity,' said Mr Pocock. 'I was hoping you'd find me a *Sterna Paradisaea*.' He laughed at Reuben's worried look. 'Arctic tern, boy. Like the common tern but with a blood-red bill, shorter legs.'

'Oh,' said Reuben. 'Right, sir.'

Mr Pocock paused. 'Had a visit from those new coastguards yesterday,' he said, startling Reuben further. 'A courtesy visit, they called it.' He shrugged. 'The officer seems decent enough but I didn't care for his second in command. Fellow called Gibbs.'

Reuben said nothing. Mr Pocock looked at him for a moment.

'Be careful, Reuben,' he said. 'All of you.'

Then he continued on his way and Reuben ran home.

Pin was not back among the lobster pots. Reuben stood by the shelter, exhaustion, disappointment and now fear bringing him close to tears. Was Pin lost, taken, run away? Had he betrayed Reuben's trust after all and peached on them?

He went indoors to find Molly with more on her mind than where her young brother-in-law had been all night. Daniel was writhing on the bed in a high fever and Molly glanced up only briefly from bathing and soothing him. Grampy was tending Francis, bouncing him gently on his shoulder.

'Take a turn, nipper,' he said, holding Francis towards Reuben.

'Did the London boy come back?' whispered Reuben, as he took the baby.

Grampy frowned. 'Bull said you went together.'

Reuben shook his head and looked away. Grampy levered himself from his chair with his stick.

'I'm due next door,' he said quietly. 'I'll tell 'em you're home safe.'

He looked hard again at Reuben, then hobbled out.

When Grampy had gone, Reuben also went out on to the beach to give Francis some air and because he felt helpless in the face of Daniel's suffering.

Bull Oliver and a group of other fishermen were sitting above the tideline, beyond the Olivers' cottage. Asher was there, and Noyce and Cotton and several others. Bull stood up and helped Grampy sit on the washed-up log he'd been occupying. Reuben knew something was being planned and longed to be in on it, but he could hardly go and join them: they'd want to know what had happened to the London boy he'd told them they could trust.

'Reuben!'

He almost dropped Francis as he turned to see Pin scrambling across the rocks from the direction of the Cormorant Cliff.

'Where have you been?' cried Reuben angrily.

'I got lost,' said Pin. 'And then I got taken by the blue-coats.'

'Taken?' Reuben's dread had instantly returned.

'Leaving Braidstone after I'd delivered the tubs.' He took the coins from his pocket and pressed them into Reuben's hand. 'Don't worry about my share,' he said.

Reuben didn't acknowledge the money.

'What d'you tell 'em?' he demanded.

'Nothin',' replied Pin, affronted. 'Nothin' at all except me name.'

'So why'd they let you go?'

'Because they couldn't prove nothin'.' Pin hesitated. 'And the officer hopes I'll spy on you.'

Reuben stared at him. 'You said you would?'

'No!' protested Pin. 'No. Course not.' He shrugged. 'I just let him think I might.'

This was too subtle for Reuben. He looked at Pin, troubled, trying to discern the truth in the London boy's face. Surely though, the five shillings he'd just been handed was proof enough that Pin hadn't changed sides? He could have kept the money and not returned. And if he had come to spy, why mention it?

Reuben shifted Francis's weight in his arms, suddenly guilty that, having accepted Pin, employed him, in fact, he was now doubting him again. He balanced Francis precariously and held out a hand.

'Thank you,' he said awkwardly.

Pin took this to mean that all was well and shook the hand.

Bull had deliberately called the meeting for when Dinah and the land crabs were visiting a cousin. Dinah had been emphatic that tonight's enterprise should be postponed. Her reasoning was good: the newly arrived blue-coats were making life in the bay too hot at the moment.

But the tide would be right, the weather calm, and Bull had already warned off the French lugger once. If it was warned off again, it might not return. The run was, as Bull had hinted to Daniel, the biggest ever into Cormorant Bay. It was Bull's venture. He knew there was a risk but he'd been ruled too much by his wife of late.

'We go tonight,' he said decisively, while others muttered around him and shook their beards like a bunch of billy goats.

'Can I take Daniel's place?'

Bull squinted up to find Reuben standing in front of him.

He grunted. 'I doubt Daniel would be coming, even if he were able, nipper.'

'Then you've all the more need of a Hibberd,' declared Reuben.

'I see. And little'un takes the helm, does he?'

Bull took Francis in one great hand and perched him on his knee.

'No,' said Reuben, feeling bolder still without a baby in his arms. 'But Pin must lend a hand too. There'll be plenty to do on the shore.'

'You know a lot about it,' growled Bull, again suddenly made more cautious by the London boy's presence. He sucked on his pipe, only to find it had gone out.

'Who's got some baccy?' he asked crossly.

Nobody had.

'I know where there's some,' said Pin impulsively.

Bull looked at him. So did everyone else.

'On the ship.' Pin nodded towards the carcase of the Calicut.

'I think not,' grunted Bull. 'We stripped her cabins clean before the blue-coats come.'

'A sailor kept a pouch on deck,' insisted Pin. 'For when he was on watch. Stuck it by the mast. I saw him.'

'Well, that won't still be there, will it,' snorted Bull. 'The sea's had that.'

Pin looked at Bull and the rest of the unloving faces a moment. It was a small thing, a pouch of tobacco, but it might finally convince Bull, if not the others. He needed Bull's approval, not just Reuben's. He turned and ran into the water.

The tide was high, the tilted wreck of the *Calicut* a sad island just offshore. It was further than it looked and very soon Pin was forced to swim. He did so like a dog, as he'd learnt when thrown into the River Thames. The style was slow, little more than treading water, but it had kept him afloat after the shipwreck long enough to find a crate to cling to. It would get him back to the *Calicut* now.

On the shore, Bull had stood up, still holding Francis, if rather absently.

'He can swim,' he murmured, stating the obvious with a certain awe in his voice.

Reuben became anxious. Swimming, like being saved, was not a high recommendation on the superstitious beach. He himself couldn't swim. But the relief he felt when Pin reached the ship was only partly because he was safe. It was also because the agility with which the London boy climbed up through the hawsehole, where the anchor had once been, drew an impressed murmur from the watching fishermen.

Pin clambered towards the stern of the ship. The hatchway to the cargo holds, through which he'd come and gone so secretly during his short career as a stowaway, gaped unsecretly before him. Beyond the hatch, the mast had gone, snapped off above its step. But between the iron rim of the step and the stump of mast still within it was a wedge of leather, salt-stained in the drying sunshine. Pin pulled it out and unwrapped it. The tobacco inside was damp but, he judged, not beyond burning.

He returned to the shore, the precious pouch clenched between his teeth, and presented it to Bull, who had unloaded Francis.

'Baccy,' he said simply, as he dripped.

'Well, thankee, boy.' Bull nodded graciously then began a gurgling laugh.

'He's still bad luck,' said Asher, cold and cutting.

Bull turned and looked him in the eye.

'P'raps strong men make their own luck,' he said.

He sat down on the log to plug his pipe with the *Calicut*'s tobacco. And offered Pin a seat beside him. Grampy shuffled sideways without complaint, and even nodded, but then he spoke.

'I'm with Dinah, Bull,' he said reluctantly. 'The blue-coats will be out again. Their breath's still on our necks.'

'They can't be everywhere,' snapped Bull.

'Then they'll certainly be here or hereabouts,' insisted Grampy.

'Not if we make sure they're somewhere else.' Reuben spoke before he'd formed the idea properly. He felt himself blushing but continued. 'If they have information, solid information that there's to be a landing at Prince's Beach or Withybank, on the other side of the Head, then that's where they'll be. Waiting for a run that never happens. While on our side of the Head, the cargo comes ashore and away, sweet and easy.'

He felt Grampy looking at him in astonishment, and wasn't sure that the old man approved of such outspoken and enthusiastic smuggling plans from his grandson. But others nodded and Bull smiled.

'I like that, nipper,' he said. 'But who's to lay the information?'

'Me, of course,' said Reuben.

Grampy looked alarmed and Bull shook his head.

'They'd not believe you,' said Bull.

'The officer believed me on Daniel's writing.'

'He believed the evidence of his own eyes,' said Bull. 'This is different. He'd smell a rat.'

There was a pause.

'I could do it.'

Pin instantly regretted the offer, but there was

no way back. He wanted acceptance. Surely this would seal it. He shrugged.

'He'd believe me. He'd expect it.'

Lieutenant Cade felt a warm spreading glow of self-satisfaction. He didn't normally allow himself such luxury, he was far too rigorous to indulge the feeling. Today was different. Today, the London boy had returned as he'd hoped – no, known – he would, but so much sooner than he could have expected. Boatman Gibbs and the rest had clearly disapproved, indeed silently scorned the lieutenant's decision to release him earlier. But here the boy was, back again the same day, thanks entirely to their chief officer's persuasive arguments.

The boy looked very nervous, more nervous even than he'd looked when brought to the coastguard station just hours ago. He glanced repeatedly at the small window, as if expecting a smuggler's threatening face to loom there and witness his act of allegiance to the rule of law.

'Prince's Beach, you say.'

'Yes, sir, definitely. At around midnight. There will be no moon and the tide will be flooding – I don't understand what that means but that's what I heard.'

Pin was trying hard not to sound like a parrot repeating the message he'd been taught.

'How many men – on the shore to receive the goods?'

'As many as ten, sir. Though I don't know their names.'

'And to bring the tubs from the lugger?'

'Four boats, sir. Four men in each.'

Lieutenant Cade silently calculated the odds. Twenty-six, maybe thirty smugglers against his six coastguards. Perhaps he should call the army to assist. But then again, he and his men would be armed and have surprise on their side. He was loath to share this early and potentially crucial success with the military. At length, he looked up and nodded.

'Your king and country are grateful to you, Pin, and you will receive a more tangible reward than words of thanks. When the rogues and their goods are captured, of course.' He smiled. 'Come to me again tomorrow and I shall give you money and arrange safe passage for you back to London. But for now, you must return to your new "friends", and do or say nothing to make them think you are an honest man.'

He stood up, walked from behind the table, and shook Pin's hand firmly, a gesture which, he felt, sealed the bond of duty between them. Then, after the boy had slipped away as quietly as he'd appeared, Lieutenant Cade strode towards the guardroom, calling as he did so.

'Boatman Gibbs! Muster the men, if you please. We have interesting work for them tonight!'

Outside, beyond the windswept gorse bushes, Pin's smile told Reuben all he needed to know. The two boys clasped hands in triumph and hurried away.

The bait had been taken.

7

Chantry Cove

The sun had set and a fresh breeze had blown away the last of a slight evening haze. The French fishermen could see the humped silhouette of the Cormorant Cliff on the horizon and began to close on it for what they hoped would be the last time. They'd been at sea for four days now, and the captain had promised that tonight they would return to Cherbourg. Whether they would be paid or not was another matter; for unless the cargo changed hands, gold and silver didn't either.

The eighty tubs, cunningly concealed beneath the deck timbers, made the boat sluggish despite the tautness of the sails in the favourable wind, but there was no great risk of being intercepted out at sea. During the war, the Channel had been thick with English warships and privateers; but the war was long since over and trade was good again. What happened to their English counterparts after the cargo was landed was not the Frenchmen's concern. All they wanted now was a smooth unloading and a swift departure with their money.

Daniel woke suddenly from a deep sleep. He was aware of the pain in his ribs; they felt as if they'd been slashed with a fish knife. But the bad smell had gone. And the nightmares. He opened his eyes and, despite the gloom, knew he was at home in his cottage. Molly was sitting beside him, Francis on her lap. She looked very tired, but smiled with relief.

Daniel's last dream came back to him: the family had been out in a boat. His lips were cracked dry but he managed to speak.

'Where's Grampy?' he asked. 'Where's Reuben?'

'Sshh . . .' said Molly, and smoothed his forehead tenderly.

Alone in the velvet darkness, high on his lookout perch, Grampy pointed the spout lantern towards France. He could no longer see the lugger but knew she would now be within lantern range. He held the lantern steady, counted to twenty, then pointed it at the ground for five seconds before raising it again and repeating the signal. The rendezvous was to be just round the point from Cormorant Bay itself, at the smaller Chantry Cove, where a recent landslide had conveniently stepped the low grassy cliff into a kind of giant's staircase, which made access far easier than the mud and ladder of Cormorant Bay.

Bull Oliver waited impatiently below, pacing the small beach of Chantry Cove, eager to be away. Then the eye of the spout lantern on the cliff above winked at him once, twice, three times and, with an excited whispered command to Asher, Noyce and Cotton, Bull ran his newly mended boat into the water and climbed aboard.

Reuben had been assigned to Asher's boat, an arrangement that pleased neither of them. But this was a time for teamwork, not personal feeling, and Reuben took up the heavy oar and concentrated on pulling hard and keeping the rhythm. Pin had played his part, now Reuben must play his.

On the beach, Pin felt momentarily alone, abandoned even. Reuben was now his friend, and Bull his champion, but the surly mistrust of the other smugglers was still evident. They kept away from him. Except for Gums, who'd already arrived with his carthorse.

'Don't worry, nipper,' he said quietly. 'They'll be drinkin' your health come mornin'.'

The French lugger was hove to a long way out and Reuben was heartily grateful when the side of the larger vessel finally loomed above him. His hands were blistered, his shoulders ached, but that didn't bother him; only the knowledge that every stroke took him into deeper and deeper water. He was scared and queasy, and desperate not to tarnish his first night as a fully fledged smuggler by being seasick.

As the small flotilla of fishing boats was secured alongside, rising and falling on the swell, Reuben could hear Bull Oliver's gruff low voice in one of the other boats, speaking to someone on board the lugger. Then the chink of a heavy bag of coin, and the much heavier clunk of wood as the first tubs were manhandled out of the lugger by the French crew.

Bull stood clinging to a line, as above him the French skipper tipped the contents of the oilcloth bag on to a platter and began carefully to count the coins. Bull could see the man's lips moving in the dim, flickering light of the lantern, held by one of the crew.

Though heavily laden, the lugger still stood high above the English fishing boats and, despite his size, Bull felt at a distinct disadvantage. He was more anxious than he'd ever been in his life. Anxious that the Frenchman might play him false. And anxious that the fishing boats might sink in the swell under the weight of the tubs. Twenty to a boat was far too many to be safe, but Bull hadn't wanted to risk making two trips out to the lugger and back, for there would be nothing to prevent the Frenchie sailing away with his money and half the paid-for cargo still on board.

It had taken Bull a long time to scrape together the funds for this run. Practically every innkeeper and farmer and parson in the county had invested in it, and they would expect their goods in return. The responsibility was squarely his and Bull had the unfamiliar feeling of having bitten off more than he could chew. Dinah was right, of course. Eighty tubs was too much, too big an enterprise. If it failed, he would be humiliated and ruined, having lost not just his own but other people's money. Rich and poor.

Then, to Bull's surprise and intense relief, the French skipper nodded down at him, and smiled.

'*Merci, monsieur. Bonne chance.*'

'Mercy, Phillipe,' replied Bull, in an awkward attempt at a foreign language. And he grinned back.

The last tubs were carefully lowered into the English boats, and lines were untied. Dinah was wrong after all, and Bull exulted as he sat down heavily and took his oar.

'Home, lads!' he called, in his loudest whisper. 'Free trade for ever!'

Then, as the lugger began to sidle away into the darkness, Reuben saw Asher handing something up to one of the crew, as he stood casting off. The exchange took only a moment, and a second later the lantern light was gone and Asher settled in the boat.

'What was that?' whispered Reuben.

Beside him, Asher took up his oar and didn't answer.

'You handed up a letter,' said Reuben, certain of what he'd seen.

'My business,' murmured Asher. 'Not yours, unless you want that nose cut off.'

Reuben began to row but he couldn't remain silent.

'The letter in Daniel's boat. Was it you that hid it there? Who wrote it?'

'Did you hear me?' demanded Asher, in quiet, deadly earnest. 'Say one word of this to anyone and I'll gut you like a mackerel.'

Grampy signalled the all-clear to the boats returning from the lugger and settled down to wait.

The night was still and silent. Or so he thought. For while the old man's lookout eyes were still sharp, many years of assault on his ears by the noise of naval cannon had left him slightly deaf. Not deaf enough to admit the defect but too deaf to hear the blue-coats creeping across the grass behind him now.

Suddenly, an arm was round his neck, a hand across his mouth, and he was flattened on his back, held, trussed and gagged. He lay mute and helpless but heard Lieutenant Cade well enough as the officer knelt beside him.

'You are not arrested,' said Lieutenant Cade calmly. 'In deference to your age and naval service. Merely snuffed out for the moment.'

Then he was gone with his men, as silently as he'd come. And Grampy was left to strain his old muscles in a futile effort to break his bonds, and rage inwardly against himself for being snuffed out. He had failed at his post.

Pin was the first of the shore party to hear the boats approaching: a definite creak and dip of oars beyond the rippling surf.

'They're back!' he whispered.

The horse beside him moved its head and Gums pulled its halter gently to keep it still. The need for silence was ingrained, even when there was no danger of discovery. Gums had tied sacking over the horse's hooves so that it would make no sound when it walked, and leave no suspicious trail of prints as it carried its load away.

The four boats ran up in line-abreast, their keels scouring deep into the shingle as they touched. And as those on board shipped oars, the shore gang ran forward to begin unloading. Pin met Reuben but didn't speak. No one spoke. Each man knew the part he had to play. Several besides Gums had brought horses, borrowed from local farmers, for they could carry four or even six tubs, where a man could carry only two, and it was vital that the cargo be shifted from the beach and hidden quickly. Each man knew a hayrick, a ploughed field, even a duck pond, where tubs could be concealed. Onward disposal could happen later.

All eighty tubs had been shifted from the boats and the loading of horses and men begun, when half a dozen lanterns suddenly lit the beach, and a loud voice cut the silence.

'Stand still. Or you will be shot!'

Pin and Reuben were momentarily blinded by the lanterns but both recognized the clear, commanding voice: Lieutenant Cade was not at Prince's Beach. He was here in Chantry Cove.

'Stand where you are!'

Only Pin and Reuben instinctively obeyed in the brief, shocked stillness. Without a word, the smugglers scattered, some running for the cliffs, some turning towards the boats.

The line of lanterns seemed to surge forward, as if bobbing on a black wave, and then gunfire flashed and burst on the boys' ears, and all around them men began to shout in anger and fear, and staid carthorses reared and squealed in panic.

On Lieutenant Cade's orders, the first volley was aimed above the smugglers' heads, but Boatman Gibbs was not one to waste powder and shot. He identified the bulk of Bull Oliver lumbering towards him, and when the thick-skulled, bellowing tide-wader was too close to miss, Boatman Gibbs squeezed the trigger with deep satisfaction.

Behind Pin and Reuben, the boats were being dragged back into the water. Noyce and Cotton were scrambling aboard, then Asher ran past and leapt after them. Suddenly, Pin lost sight of Reuben, and as he looked frantically around in the confusion, a horse backed into him and knocked him flat, and he lay on his face in the damp, churned-up sand with his hands protecting his head, while terrified men and horses trod and stumbled over him.

Wriggling backwards on his stomach, Pin felt wet shingle beneath his toes, then the sea itself washing over his ankles. He kept going until a wave covered his shoulders, striking cold against his neck, then he turned and crawled away through the surf, abreast of the beach, like an ungainly sea creature. Around him, men splashed and fell into the water, trying to reach the departing boats, as more gunfire crackled. There was no sign of Reuben.

Pin stayed low in the water. Eventually, his hands and knees struck rocks and he realized he had reached the tumbled edge of the cove and the narrow finger of cliff which separated it from

Cormorant Bay. He groped his way from rock to rock towards the point, kicking off the heavy swaying kelp that wrapped itself invisibly round his legs, trying to hold him back until the blue-coats could come and take him.

The gunfire had petered out, and Pin could hear no shouting now. Did that mean the smugglers had all escaped? Or were dead? Where was Reuben? Pin hauled himself out of the water and began to shiver.

Lieutenant Cade strode to the water's edge and peered vainly out to sea. It had all been over quickly. Not like a naval engagement where, once grappled, the enemy must fight to the death or surrender. This enemy was slippery. The boats had vanished. Even those smugglers who had run for the cliffs had got away. His only captives were three carthorses but, though disappointed, Lieutenant Cade was not distraught. His men had been steady. He was glad not to have set the precedent of sharing success with the army. For there was some success: the smugglers had escaped but they had done so empty-handed. Their entire cargo of eighty tubs lay on the beach behind him. Lieutenant Cade had made his mark.

'What shall we do with the body, sir?'

Boatman Gibbs's almost casual enquiry stung him and he clenched his fists before turning to reply. The smugglers had been unarmed, apart from a discarded cudgel or two. Bull Oliver could have been restrained without a ball between the eyes. Not that Lieutenant Cade would admit as much, should Gibbs ever face a judge and jury.

'Return it to his wife,' he said tersely. 'Find a cart.'

Grampy had heard the shouting and the gunfire, and the sounds had tortured him.

None of the fleeing smugglers came within sight until, of all people, the London boy appeared over the cliff edge and, seeing Grampy, stopped and crouched, staring at him in the dim, pre-dawn light, before hurrying forward and starting to untie his wrists.

Every second since being captured, Grampy had been working at the cloth gag in his mouth with his few remaining teeth, and the sight of the London boy made him chew all the harder, though his jaws ached enough to crack. The boy had deceived him, deceived them all. There was no knowing who was alive or dead on the beach below, but there had been an ambush and the boy must have arranged it.

Suddenly, Grampy spat and spluttered and the frayed sodden gag fell from his mouth.

'Keep away from me, you little squealer!'

'I never squealed, Grampy! I never! I said Prince's Beach, not Chantry Cove!'

But Pin could hear his own voice. It sounded horribly unconvincing, a pleading whine.

'Squealer!' cried Grampy. 'Double-dealer! Rat! Peacher! Two-spotted dog!'

His hands were free now and he at least had the satisfaction of catching the boy a flailing blow across the face and seeing him run off like a dog. A craven wild dog, running from the pack he had sought to destroy.

Pin didn't stop running till he was on the Cormorant Cliff. There, he threw himself into the great crack in the turf where he and Reuben had hidden the tubs, and lay there sobbing. He gouged handfuls of the soft chalky soil, as if by doing so he could somehow recapture the moment when he'd first proved his worth to the people of Cormorant Bay. When acceptance and trust had begun. Now, bewilderingly, that trust, that starting to belong, had been snatched away. Pin was an outsider again, driven out. Worse, he was now an enemy. And likely to be hunted.

8

Burial

Dinah knew before it arrived what was in the cart.

She should have raged and cursed, she supposed. Flown with tears and nails at the stiffly upright officer standing at her door. But she merely nodded and said nothing, and watched as the blue-coats heaved her husband's body into the cottage. Though she did take a quiet pride in the fact that it needed four of them to lift him.

'I shall be making a full written report of the incident to my superiors,' said Lieutenant Cade, speaking as stiffly as he stood. 'You are, of course, at liberty to take up the matter with them. Or with the civil authorities. However, I should tell you, if you do not already know, that your husband was undoubtedly engaged in a smuggling run. And violently resisted arrest.'

He wondered if she would 'take up the matter', despite this heavy hint that it would do no good. Probably not. Not through official channels, at least. These people had as little to do with official channels as possible. Retribution was another matter, though. He could not tell what the woman was thinking but he feared that she, or others, would already be planning revenge. Boatman Gibbs was likely to prove not just a liability but a deadly one.

'Shall I call the parson for you, ma'm?' he asked, still scrupulously polite.

Dinah shook her head. 'No,' she said. 'We don't have no truck with religion.'

'Your husband must be properly buried. Once the legalities have been completed.'

'He will be,' she said. 'Thank you for returning him.'

She turned away into the cottage and shut the door.

As Lieutenant Cade remounted his horse and rode away, he thought briefly of the London boy. He doubted he would see him again. Assuming he was still alive.

Dinah didn't blame the blue-coats for her husband's death. Bull had always known the risks of the trade and faced them. She sat quietly beside him now, while her children peered down, frightened, from the attic above. After a while, Dinah looked up at them and called huskily, 'Come and say goodbye to your father.'

*

Reuben watched from the rocks where he'd first met Pin, as the blue-coats trundled away with their cart. He'd seen the body and was shocked. In the gunfire and chaos of last night, he hadn't known that Bull had fallen. Hadn't known anything except that they'd been ambushed. He'd lost contact with Pin and then it had been every man for himself. Frantic, inglorious escape. He'd been finally creeping home when he'd seen the blue-coats arrive at the Olivers' cottage. Now, he hurried on.

'Reuben! Reuben!'

Molly embraced him tearfully. Daniel was sitting up with Francis in his arms, but before Reuben could say how good it was to see his brother on the mend, Grampy snarled at him from his chair beside the hearth.

'That London weasel's done for us. Bull's dead because of him!'

Reuben stood staring at his grandfather, utterly stunned. The thought had truly not occurred to him. Not even now.

'Pin would not do that. We saved him. He's our friend. He wouldn't squeal on us.'

Reuben looked from Grampy to the rest of his silent family.

'What've you done with him?' he cried in sudden fear.

'He's run away,' said Molly.

Reuben couldn't tell what she believed of Pin,

nor what Daniel thought but Grampy spat into the fire.

'And he'd better not come back,' he growled.

Reuben ran from the house.

Pin had fallen asleep where he lay, his fists still clutching chalky dirt, the growing warmth of the sun on his back soothing him.

Reuben had almost given up the search when he finally found him. He was so relieved that he sat for a few moments on the edge of the great crack in the turf and flicked small snail shells at Pin to wake him gently. He was not aware that he'd been seen leaving home. And followed.

Pin woke and saw Reuben looking down at him. He sat up and shrank away, expecting accusations and abuse.

'I said Prince's Beach. Prince's Beach. Not Chantry Cove.'

'It's all right, Pin.' Reuben spoke quickly to reassure him. 'I know you never squealed. Someone must've gone to the blue-coats after you did. Someone who knew the plan.' He held out his hand. 'Come out of there.'

Pin still regarded him warily.

'Pin, are we true friends or not?'

Reuben sounded aggrieved now. He was about to take his hand away when Pin grabbed it. But as Pin hauled himself out on to the grass, his wariness became alarm and, seeing his face change, Reuben turned.

Asher was marching towards them over the hump of the down. Noyce and Cotton were with him, and half a dozen others.

'See?' said Asher, with a vindicated smirk at his companions as they approached. 'Thick as herrings in a barrel. Stand up!' he ordered.

Reuben and Pin did so slowly, Reuben ready to protect his friend. But to his surprise, Asher dismissed Pin.

'The ship's rat can go,' he snapped. 'Let him scurry back to London. You're the one we want. You're the cause of all our troubles. Hold him!'

And he took off the coil of rope that was looped across his shoulder.

Reuben kicked and fought, and Pin threw himself at Asher, but Cotton dragged him off and kicked him away. Coins were thrown at him, not in generosity but with vicious intent, together with curses and jeers.

'Take your reward and go!'

A coin cut his forehead and he fell, then scrambled away beyond a bank of gorse.

Reuben was being held on the ground now, his hands and ankles tied.

'You and the London boy was in it together,' declared Asher. ''Twas you that squealed.'

'That ain't so!' cried Reuben, outraged but

frightened now as he struggled vainly and felt the rope bite.

'Nothin' simpler,' said Asher. 'You went there with him. To the coastguard station.'

'Hibberds ain't traitors!' protested Reuben, trying to stop his voice from shaking. 'Why should I do such a thing?'

'Don't play stupid,' said Asher, pulling the rope tighter still. 'For the reward, o' course. How much did you get?'

'What reward?'

'There's always a reward for information,' continued Asher easily, 'and you Hibberds are always pleadin' poverty. Poor but above 'emselves, eh?'

He glanced up at his companions and received a grumble of agreement.

'What with Daniel bein' too holy for the trade, and his readin' and writin'. And yours.'

''Twas you put that letter in Daniel's boat!' shouted Reuben. 'So's it wouldn't be found on you!'

But nobody was interested.

'You sold us, nipper.' Asher was emphatic. 'And that sly old salt of a grandfather was in on it too. Givin' the false all-clear from the clifftop.'

Reuben was shocked to hear resentment and rising anger all around him.

'That's a lie! Don't listen to him!' he cried.

134

'You're the liar, boy,' said Asher, standing over him. 'It's cos of you that Bull is dead, and the cargo lost, and all manner of ills come upon us since you fished that London rat from his rightful grave. Isn't that so, boys?'

The agreement was wholehearted now, and vengeful.

'And there's only one way to make things right,' continued Asher. He crouched, his face close to Reuben's. 'You must pay your debt.'

He pulled Reuben up and threw him over his shoulder, then carried him off.

The rest of the gang cheered and marched alongside. Reuben managed to raise his head and look backwards, his eyes desperately scanning the sweep of the down for a hope of rescue. But no band of blue-coats came galloping towards him, no villager appeared. And Pin, it seemed, had gone.

Dinah's fingers were stiff and sore from sewing sailcloth, but she felt a moment of deep sadness when the job was done.

After a few seconds gazing at her handiwork, she got up and went outside into the sunshine. Her land crabs were waiting in a solemn obedient group, having pushed their father's boat down to the water's edge.

The boat had been returned by Asher and a few of the other men, but they'd seemed more intent on blame and revenge than respect for the dead. Dinah didn't want their assistance now, nor did she seek help from the Hibberds. She and her children had said their goodbyes. It was enough. She was impatient. No 'legalities'. She wanted to bury her husband now, while the sun was dancing on the water. He alone of his community had truly loved the sea. All the others feared, hated or merely used it. Bull had been different. Right now, the sea was welcoming: it called her. And it called her husband. Dinah and her children eased the great sailcloth bundle from the table, then half carrying, half dragging, conveyed it to the waiting boat.

Pin lay as close as he dared to the cliff edge. Below him, the small knot of men was clambering over the rocks. He could see Reuben being carried like a rolled-up carpet. Pin wriggled forward as the gang disappeared from view but, in his eagerness to see, he dislodged a small cluster of chalk and dusty roots and had to retreat swiftly in case someone looked up.

Nobody did. All were intent on the matter in hand. It was painful for Reuben to turn his head, having been jolted upside down for so long, but he could see that the tide was out; that the rocks were dark, dank, slime-covered, while the cliff, close on his right, had the grey green stain of the tide along it. He'd been brought below the high-water mark.

Finally, Asher jumped down on to a tiny beach, a gash of sand and shingle between soaring chalk and a long barrier of sea rock. And Reuben realized their destination: Black Tooth.

Asher strode down on to the hard glistening sand before the cave's mouth and briefly studied the thin thread of surf creeping in past Sun Rock. He shrugged off Reuben and dug his heel into the sand.

'Here!' he called.

Now, for the first time, Reuben noticed that one of the other smugglers, Noyce, was carrying a short-handled spade. He tried to give it away but no one would take it.

'Dig, damn you!' said Asher fiercely. 'We're all agreed and we're all in this together. Every man shall take a turn.'

Noyce began to dig, and the hole in the wet sand in front of Reuben deepened rapidly. Once Noyce had started it, others became more willing to take a turn, and each dug more swiftly than the last.

Those not digging stood with arms folded, staring implacably at Reuben. They had made up their minds and would see it through now. Whether or not it was Reuben himself who'd betrayed them to the blue-coats, as Asher insisted, no longer mattered. He had cheated the sea and brought disaster. This was the only way to put things right.

The hole was soon finished, and though he wriggled and writhed like one of the reddish-brown lugworms the digging had thrown up, Reuben was dragged feet-first into it.

There was water in the bottom, cold and gritty, but the sand shovelled back in quickly soaked up the moisture as it compacted itself round Reuben's feet and ankles, then his knees, then waist. He had set his heart against pleading. Grampy wouldn't plead, nor Daniel and nor would he. But it was hard when you were terrified.

'Each man shall take a turn,' reiterated Asher, thrusting the spade at one of the smugglers who was hanging back, but he reserved the final spadeful for himself, throwing it against Reuben's neck, then firming it down with his feet, so that the sand held Reuben as if in an iron fist, a fist still closing, crushing the breath from him.

Asher squatted in front of the condemned boy and gave him an unpleasant little smile of triumph.

'Any last words?' he asked.

With a supreme effort, Reuben looked Asher in the eye, then shook his head.

Asher laughed, threw a handful of wet sand at Reuben's face, stood up and turned away.

He led the smugglers back the way they'd come, leaving only a boy's head visible on the sand.

Pin was on the shore now. He could see a fishing boat being rowed laboriously out across the bay. The crew were tiny, and in the bows was something large and bulky, protruding like a figurehead.

He heard the smugglers returning and dived behind a great boulder, his feet slipping into a rock pool. He stood as still as he could, while small fish nibbled his toes. The gang passed by, but Reuben wasn't with them. Had he escaped? Pin didn't think so; the men were talking quietly. He waited as long as his patience held out, then crept onwards.

The warm sunshine on the sheltered beach had brought out the flies. They settled on Reuben's face, as if knowing he was powerless to swat them away. He shook his head repeatedly, like a tormented animal, but they always returned, crawling into his ears and nose and mouth.

Reuben had been buried facing the sea, so that he could watch the tide, now turned, creeping slowly but inexorably up the beach towards him.

From time to time, he made a supreme effort to break free, but whichever technique he tried – wriggling, stretching, pushing with his knees – made no difference. He could gain no leverage. It was as if he were set in stone.

As soon as he'd thought the smugglers themselves must be out of earshot, he had started shouting for help. Nothing had happened, though, except that he'd choked on the flies and lost his voice for several minutes and the pale green wavelets had whispered mockingly in reply as they lapped ever closer.

Dinah stopped rowing and gazed back at the distant cottages. This was far enough. The whole arc of Cormorant Bay embraced her. She nodded and, after a brief hesitation, her children scrambled forward. The entire family heaved together, and with a heavy splash, the long, stone-weighted bundle was pushed overboard. It sank, ghostly white beneath the surface, then disappeared into the dark blue deep.

'Rest in peace, Bull,' said Dinah.

Pin had scrambled all the way to Black Tooth without finding Reuben. The small beach was empty too, and there was no way past. He must look in the cave itself. He started towards it, then stopped. There *was* something on the beach. Something outside the cave: small, dark and round, moving from side to side, yet not moving at all. A rippling wave reached it and it shook itself violently as if distressed and cried out.

Pin stared, slowly realizing what he'd found. Horrified, he raced towards it.

The wave hadn't broken over Reuben, but curled some ten paces away and run up the beach, low, swift and exultant. It hissed in his ears as it sank into the sand round his neck, and its cold wetness settled on his buried shoulders.

The next engulfed him, filling his ears with a deep steady roar that Reuben assumed must be the last thing you heard before drowning. But as the wave slid back past him, something grabbed his shoulder and he cried out as he choked on sand and salt water, thinking a sea monster must already have claimed him.

'It's me!' shouted Pin, but he could make no impact pushing and pulling Reuben's shoulders, nor when he tried to get his hands beneath them. He cursed the feebleness of his own arms and collapsed in the next swirling wave that swept over them both. He tried scrabbling at the wet sand, digging like a dog, but that seemed to make no difference either. Then he looked up, and through tears of frustration glimpsed the fishing boat again. Out beyond Sun Rock. He yelled as loudly as he could, staggered to his feet and waved his arms frantically. The boat disappeared. He looked at Reuben, at his hopeless efforts to save him, then turned and splashed away into the rising tide.

Pin climbed the craggy flank of Sun Rock itself, clawing his way upwards past flapping seabirds, and finally balancing precariously on its ridge, from where he could see the boat again. It was full of Olivers. He shouted and waved. Still there seemed to be no reaction. Pin was screaming now, and suddenly the boat began to turn. As it did, Pin toppled backwards, plummeting thirty feet into the channel behind him.

He was lucky to miss the submerged rocks that would have broken his back but had no time to dwell on his own good fortune. He struggled to Reuben again and fell to his knees, digging frantically once more, flinging sand behind him, and continuing to do so even when his efforts were inundated. Inadvertently, the sea helped a little now by washing away the loosened sand so that Reuben's shoulders became visible and Pin could get his hands beneath his armpits. He tried hauling again but nothing happened. It was still not enough and as Reuben retched and spluttered, Pin looked desperately towards Sun Rock, willing the Olivers' boat to appear. They'd seen his signal and turned towards him, so where were they? When the boat did appear, painfully slowly, Pin ran into the surf to drag it ashore. The Olivers were gazing, appalled, at Reuben's head.

'Help me!' cried Pin.

He splashed back to the buried boy, and Dinah suddenly came to life and scrambled out of the boat after him.

The land crabs quickly followed, and with their help Pin burrowed deeper, while Dinah hauled at Reuben's arms and wished she had the strength of her husband.

'Hold up his head!' she yelled at her children as Reuben's face disappeared under water again, then wildly, 'Save the boat!' as she saw it suddenly floating where they had beached it. And two of them ran to catch the rope and pull the boat back on the next wave.

Suddenly, Reuben felt that he could breathe more easily and move his chest and shoulders, and the more he moved, the more the sea undid itself by washing out the sand that held him. Kneeling beside him, Dinah groped down in the boggy sand until she felt his wrists and the rope that bound them.

'Fetch the fish knife!' she cried, and a land crab obediently dashed back to the boat.

Probing carefully with the keen-edged blade, Dinah sawed at the rope until the strands parted. Now at last Reuben could help his rescuers, squirming his arms free so that he could use his hands to lever himself upwards. With the others still digging and heaving, he gradually hauled himself from his living, cloying grave. Dinah cut the rope that held his feet and, as Reuben staggered upright, the subsiding hole was engulfed again and this time stayed covered. He knew that if he'd been trapped a minute longer, he would have remained submerged, only his hair visible like a tuft of swaying seaweed.

Pin and Dinah helped Reuben to the boat and he lay in the stern, shocked, exhausted and encrusted with sand, while they struggled against the tide with the oars, and the children fended off rocks as the boat swayed and bumped its way out of the channel and turned for home.

Once they were safely clear of Sun Rock, Dinah gave her outrage full rein.

'Who did this to you?' she demanded.

'Asher,' croaked Reuben.

'There was eight or nine of 'em,' said Pin, eager to denounce. 'They reckoned it was Reuben squealed to the blue-coats about the run. And they said he must pay for rescuing me from the shipwreck.'

''Tis barbaric,' muttered Dinah. 'They'll answer to your family and to me.'

'I can't go home yet,' said Reuben quickly.

'Why ever not?'

'Because Pin can't. It's not safe for him. Put us ashore where you can, please, Dinah.'

Dinah began to protest but Reuben became agitated.

'Please, Dinah. Tell my family I'm safe – that you saved me – but let us ashore. Please.'

Dinah glared at them both. Pin said nothing,

because he wasn't sure what he should say. Then Dinah swung the boat towards the rocks and when it grounded, Reuben scrambled gratefully ashore, with Pin following.

'They'll still answer to me,' promised Dinah, darkly, as she pushed the boat off again. 'Take care.'

Reuben perched on the rocks in silence. Pin sat beside him, watching the Olivers' boat pull slowly away. By the time it had reached the cottages, the weather had changed completely. A thick rolling mist had turned the sea a turbid grey, and the sun, so warm and cheering minutes earlier, was reduced to a pale disc, glimpsed occasionally through the gloom.

Reuben shivered in the sudden chill. He stood up, turned to Pin and shrugged.

'That finally makes us even, I suppose. A life for a life.'

Pin shrugged too. 'Don't mean you have to stay away from your family,' he said. 'Not on my account. You don't have to stay with me.'

'No,' agreed Reuben. 'And nor do you with me. You can leave now, if you like.'

Pin shook his head. 'I must stay till you're recovered enough to take a punch on the nose.'

Reuben looked surprised. 'For what?'

'The invisible babies. That are only lambs.'

Reuben grinned. 'I'm sorry.'

145

'You will be.'

Reuben was silent again, then looked up at Pin, serious now.

'But first,' he said, 'for both our sakes, we must find out who *did* peach.'

Boatman Gibbs surveyed the sweep of Cormorant Bay as if he owned it. He didn't mind the sea mist. Others found it depressing or eerie, certainly dangerous, but being fearless, Boatman Gibbs was never bothered by the weather.

Lieutenant Cade had excused Gibbs from the tiresome duty of lugging the captured tubs up from Chantry Cove. A wagon had been brought to convey the contraband to the Customs House at Alvershill but Gibbs had been sent away from the scene before the task began. He knew well enough that this was a rebuke rather than a reward: that in Lieutenant Cade's opinion, his continued presence at the scene of Bull Oliver's death might further inflame local feeling. Boatman Gibbs viewed such concerns with contempt, but in practical terms it suited him. He would much rather patrol than load a wagon. He was a coastguard, not a porter.

The mist rose from the sea below like smoke from some great fire, and through it Gibbs saw two figures in a hollow by the cliff edge. Skulking, whispering. Plotting, in all likelihood.

Gibbs crept closer but, in his excitement, moved too fast and his quarry heard him. A voice he knew spoke out.

'Boatman Gibbs, is that you?'

The figure that spoke was holding a short stick. Then the stick flashed orange and Boatman Gibbs had a split second of life to realize it wasn't a stick after all, before he fell backwards, with the bang fading in his ears.

9

The Rifle

'Stupid young fool . . .' muttered Grampy. He was cold and damp and he hated fog.

'At least he's loyal to his friends,' said Daniel, who had insisted on looking for Reuben. It was many hours now since he'd run out of the house.

Grampy sniffed. In truth, he was feeling bad about his own violent reaction to the London boy, and was secretly proud that Reuben had defended him. But he had no more idea than Daniel where the two of them might have gone. Hobbling about on the clifftop seemed to him a futile exercise.

'You're not well enough to be out here,' he grumbled. 'You'll split your wound open again.'

He stopped to ease the ache in his good leg, peering down into the opaque greyness that hid the sea, and hoped that Dinah and her land crabs had returned safely ashore.

Thankfully, the mist was starting to thin, the late afternoon sun burning an orange hole in it, and Grampy could better see the cracks and hollows lying in wait for his walking stick. Daniel had walked on but now Grampy saw him stop at the edge of a deep gully near the cliff edge.

Daniel turned to him and shouted. 'Here! Quickly!' then disappeared into the gully.

Grampy hurried after him and when he reached the edge, flung aside his stick and slid on his backside down past the rows of rabbit holes on to the hard rough chalk at the bottom of the gully.

Daniel was crouching beside a body.

'No . . .' groaned Grampy, scrambling forward in fear. But though Daniel's face was pale as he turned, he shook his head.

'It's Boatman Gibbs,' he said quietly.

Grampy stared. 'Is he dead?'

Daniel nodded, wiping his hand in the dirt.

'Shot?'

'It would seem so.'

'I thought I heard a gun an hour ago,' said Grampy, 'but I don't trust me ears no more.'

The two men stayed crouched in silence. Boatman Gibbs was no loss to their world, but his death had not been accidental.

Daniel suddenly looked up, at first feeling rather than hearing hoof beats. He got to his feet, peering beyond the top of the gully. A group of horsemen was approaching, silhouetted against the now dazzling sun.

Grampy hauled himself up on Daniel's arm.

There was no time to flee, even if he'd had two feet to run with; and his stick still lay on the grass above. The horsemen trampled to a halt at the edge of the gully. Blue-coats.

Lieutenant Cade swiftly dismounted from his great black horse, unsheathing his sword as he took in the scene below him: the two beach-dwellers and the sprawled inert body. A uniformed body that he clearly recognized. Other blue-coats were dismounting, drawing pistols. They followed Lieutenant Cade as he skidded down into the gully.

Daniel tried to remain calm but cursed himself for having seen the body in the first place.

'What is this?' asked Lieutenant Cade.

'A dead man,' replied Daniel. 'We've just come upon him.'

'Just come upon him,' echoed Lieutenant Cade. 'You have blood on you.'

'I felt for a heartbeat,' explained Daniel.

Lieutenant Cade stooped, examining the bloody mess of Gibbs's jacket, then put aside his sword and crouched beside the body, ripping open the jacket and the shirt beneath to reveal the gunshot wound itself.

'And the weapon?' he asked.

Daniel shrugged. 'There's none here, as you can well see.'

'Then you've disposed of it?' Lieutenant Cade signalled to his men and they dispersed along the gully, climbing to the cliff edge to scan the rocks below.

'I'm a fisherman,' said Daniel. 'I use a net, not a gun.'

'You also scavenge wrecks.' Lieutenant Cade looked up. 'There were rifles on the *Calicut*. One case is missing. Twelve weapons.'

'I did not take them.'

'Someone did. A boy from here tried to sell one in Alvershill.'

Grampy felt Daniel start slightly. Lieutenant Cade noticed and was pleased.

'The guns were on their way to India,' he continued. 'A new model, to be tested by the army. And the ammunition is specific to them. It cannot be used in any other kind of rifle.' He tapped Boatman Gibbs's chest beside the blackened hole. 'So, when the surgeon removes this shot, we shall know what we shall know.'

'You will not know I shot him,' protested Daniel, but he sensed a determination about the officer now.

'I know that a jury may decide you did,' retorted Lieutenant Cade, as he straightened up. 'You are here, red-handed, beside the victim. And you had a clear motive: a dozen people must have heard you threaten Gibbs. I am disappointed, Hibberd: I showed you mercy. You repay me with murder. For this crime, yes, I think you *will* hang.'

He turned to his men. They had found no weapon, but Lieutenant Cade did not consider it essential.

'Take him away,' he ordered. 'And hand the old man down his stick.'

'Reuben! Blue-coats!' warned Pin. And they scurried into the cover of a blackthorn hedge.

The coastguards trotted by, but there was one rider with them who was not wearing a blue coat. A prisoner.

Once the horsemen had gone, Reuben turned slowly to Pin, hoping to be told he was mistaken.

'Was that Daniel?' he whispered.

Pin could only nod.

Dinah made the tea as strong as tar and shovelled in a scandalous amount of sugar.

'Drink it down, lovey,' she said, and held the bowl herself as Molly took it with shaking fingers and tried to swallow.

Molly looked awful, which was hardly surprising.

'Reuben's alive,' reiterated Dinah, sitting beside Molly, but still holding the bowl to the girl's lips. 'However wicked what was done to him, he's alive. And the London boy's with him. They'll be all right.'

'He'd be home now if we hadn't driven Pin

away. It's our fault!' Molly pushed the tea from her and began to sob again, then turned abruptly as she heard the back door scrape open and the sound of Grampy's stick.

'There you are,' said Dinah, with a relieved smile. 'They're all back safe.'

But only Grampy appeared, exhausted and grimly anxious. Molly stood up.

'What now?' she asked fearfully. 'Grampy?'

'Daniel's taken for murder,' said the old man, and he collapsed in his chair.

The beach was deserted but Reuben told Pin to wait in the shelter. He hurried on to the cottage, his heart thumping. Perhaps he was wrong: Daniel would be here.

As soon as he slipped indoors, he knew the worst. He could see Molly pacing, rocking Francis in her arms for comfort.

'It's not just. It's not right. They've been set against my Daniel from the start. But how can they think he'd commit a murder?'

She looked up and the sight of Reuben caused her to dissolve. Dinah hurried forward to comfort her again and Reuben looked bewilderedly at Grampy.

'Boatman Gibbs has been shot,' said the old man. 'Me and Daniel found him. The blue-coats found us.'

He shrugged, momentarily defeated, and returned his gaze to the smoky fire.

'Reuben,' said Molly urgently. 'You must go for help.'

'Help?' scoffed Grampy. 'Who's to help the likes of us against the law?'

'Important people,' said Molly. 'Squire Coleman, Mr Pocock – Parson Teague.'

Grampy snorted.

'Of course they would!' cried Molly, becoming wild in her desperation. 'They're all subscribers to the trade. They'd speak up for any shore folk.'

'What, openly defend a smuggler?' answered Grampy. 'Molly, they're hypocrites to a man! They'd shut the door on us.'

At which Molly burst into tears of despair and Grampy at once regretted his brutal honesty and put his arm round her, while Dinah took the baby. When he looked up from his shushing and gentle apologies, Grampy's eyes met Reuben's, and he gave a bleak little nod. 'Off you go,' he said softly.

'Where are we going?' whispered Pin.

'Parsonage,' replied Reuben, as he climbed the ladder from the beach.

Pin was surprised. 'To get your pound for the drowned bodies?'

'No,' said Reuben. 'Someone's shot Boatman

Gibbs. Molly says the parson'll stop 'em hangin' Daniel for it.'

But their welcome was as chilly as the stone hallway in which they were received.

'I am not a lawyer,' said Parson Teague. 'I'm a man of God.'

'Well, yes, sir,' said Reuben, struggling to remember the Bible class he'd once attended. 'Daniel's in your flock, and the wolf's taken him.'

'Don't be profane,' snapped the parson. 'Your brother was never once in my church. However, if he desires to make confession . . .'

'But he never done it, sir!'

'Then he has nothing to fear. His soul is safe.'

They were shown the door.

Reuben wanted to mention the letter. He was worried that it would in some way now be used against his brother.

'The blue-coats have a letter,' he said quickly, 'that was put in Daniel's boat. It's from a Disciple. Are you a Disciple, sir?'

Parson Teague stared down at him.

'Go home, you foolish boy,' he said. 'And pray.'

There was no help at the manor house, either. Squire Coleman's dogs, let loose in the grounds at evening, prevented them from even reaching the door.

So, as a last resort, Reuben ran up the winding lane to Marine View, the house on the cliff where Mr Pocock lived, explaining breathlessly to Pin as they went that Mr Pocock was not a lawyer, but not a man of God either, so he might listen. He came from London, so Pin might have met him. He was old and rich and paid good money for seabirds, though you had to be careful how you killed them because he didn't like damage.

But Mr Pocock was a disappointment too. No more help than the stuffed birds that stared out from inside their glass domes, while Reuben gabbled out his story and Pin tried not to muddy the polished floor of the display room.

Mr Pocock was shocked to hear of the two deaths, and of Daniel's arrest. He sighed and tutted and nodded sympathetically and, when Reuben had finished, he agreed that things looked bad. Very bad.

'D'you not know the magistrate at Alvershill?' asked Reuben hopefully.

Mr Pocock shrugged. 'I knew the old one, but not the new. Besides, it's not the magistrate that hangs people. It's a judge and jury. And probably in London.'

'London?' Reuben was appalled. 'They'll take Daniel all the way up there?'

'I should think it likely.'

'Then we must free him before they can!' cried

Reuben. 'We must make an army, and take weapons and break open the gaol!'

'Then you will *all* hang,' warned Mr Pocock.

He looked gravely at the agitated boy and spoke with genuine regret.

'I'm sorry, Reuben. I cannot approve such a plan.'

It started to rain as they left Marine View: a heavy rain, driving in from the west. Despite it, Reuben didn't want to go straight home. There was the risk of meeting Asher and others of the gang, but mainly he felt he couldn't destroy Molly's hopes. He'd failed to secure help from those she'd thought would offer it. Perhaps he'd think of something else.

'Let's shelter in the Nest,' he said and trudged away.

The elder trees and nettles gave protection of a kind from the rain, and the crate of rifles was still there beneath the bracken.

The boys huddled against the crate, pulled the bracken over themselves and spent the remainder of the wretched evening staring out at the weather in silence.

Reuben was aghast when he realized he'd been asleep. There was no sun, only a uniformly leaden sky from which the rain lashed down even more energetically than before, but morning had definitely arrived. He crawled quickly from the

Nest. He must go home, with or without good news. His family would be sick with worry again by now.

Only when Pin had scrambled out beside him, did Reuben notice what he hadn't realized in the dark: a rifle was missing – his rifle. The one he'd put back in the Nest, but not in the crate, after his foolhardy attempt to sell it.

Reuben knelt and pulled out the crate, pushing aside the lid and quickly counting the guns inside to be certain. Eleven.

Pin was watching him. 'What's the matter?' he asked.

'There's a rifle missing. I put it back – it's gone again.'

For a moment, the fruitless evening, the uncomfortable night and a hunger that would no longer be subdued by finer feelings got the better of Pin.

'Well,' he grunted. 'P'raps Daniel shot the blue-coat, after all.'

'Don't you dare say that!'

Reuben turned with startling savagery and slammed Pin's head back against the wooden crate, holding him by the shoulders as he glowered down at him.

'My brother's not a murderer. Nor a liar.' He banged Pin's head again.

'All right!' cried Pin. 'I'm sorry. I only said perhaps.'

'You'd never say even that about your own brother!'

'I 'aven't got one.'

Pin found the ferocious family loyalty both strange and enviable.

'I'm sorry,' he repeated, and meant it.

Reuben paused, then let him go, and Pin raised his head painfully. But as Reuben replaced the lid on the crate, he stopped again, staring at it.

'Pin, look,' he said urgently, his anger quite forgotten.

Pin twisted round and gazed at the wooden lid. He frowned. 'What?'

Reuben pointed at a barely visible chalk cross scrawled on it.

'This mark,' he said. 'It's like on one of the tubs – when they was hidden up on the cliff? Gums has been here!'

They found Gums in the shepherd's hut, which smelt strongly of wet sheepdog. Gums was sitting on the floor, methodically tugging burrs from his dog's coat, while eating a breakfast of stale bread and even harder cheese.

'Here y'are, nipper,' he said, generously offering a lump of cheese to Pin. 'Try a bit of local. Mind yer teeth, though. 'Tis better with a saw to cut it.'

Pin accepted but Reuben shook his head to cheese.

'Gums, did you find a crate of rifles up behind Toogood's? Did you take one?'

Gums concentrated on the burrs. 'Parson's back,' he said.

'Forget the parson,' said Reuben, with an edge. 'Rifles. Behind the elder trees and nettles.'

'Well,' said Gums, 'me and the old girl always has our eyes open, as you know.' He patted the dog and looked up at Reuben. 'We seen you two plantin' tubs t'other mornin'.' He shrugged. 'Never said a word. Left me mark. Waited. Went back. Nothin'. Silence is supposed to have a certain value, y'know.' He sniffed, offended. 'Better a friend comes across what's been planted than a blue-coat. There shoulda been a thank you.'

'The rifles, Gums!' cried Reuben, exasperated.

Gums shrugged again and returned his attention to the patient dog, raking a matted ball of hair and sorrel seeds from her coat with a greasy comb.

''Twas the old girl,' he said. 'She was in round the nettles and I seed they was trampled down. And she were sniffin' and sniffin' at this pile o' bracken, so I give it a tug, and blow me . . .'

'You took a rifle.'

Gums looked up and nodded, unashamed.

'I did. I was owed a tub, so I left me mark and took one o' they instead.'

'You know it's been used for murder,' said

Reuben. He didn't mean it to sound like an accusation.

Gums stared at him, his entire absence of teeth visible, then looked at Pin, who was gnawing vainly at the cheese, as if he might say otherwise.

'Daniel's been taken for it,' continued Reuben, pressing. 'Gums, what happened to the rifle?'

Gums found his voice and rallied. 'Why, I sold it. As you was set to do, no doubt. And with a box o' cartridges for good measure.'

'Who to, Gums?' demanded Reuben. 'For Daniel's sake, tell me!'

Gums looked away and pulled the fur ball from the comb.

'Asher give me ten shillun for it.'

It was the last name Reuben wanted to hear.

The quickest way to Asher's house was over the down and along the Cormorant Cliff, almost as far as the cottages on the beach below, before turning up the lane towards the church. At least the rain was at their backs now, and the distance gave Reuben time to think.

Perhaps Asher would be so shocked to see him risen from his grave of sand and seawater that he'd fall at Reuben's feet and confess everything. On the other hand, perhaps he would merely shoot him. And Pin as well.

Pin expected the latter outcome.

'What about the blue-coats?' he asked. 'Wouldn't that be better? Tell them who's got the rifle.'

But Reuben had no more faith than Grampy in authority, especially in the form of Lieutenant Cade. And there was no one else to turn to now. He and Pin must manage as they could.

The tide was not yet full but the south-westerly wind was piling the sea into Cormorant Bay below them. Billowing waves, yellow-grey and seething white, were breaking over the half-submerged hulk of the *Calicut*, and already licking close to the cottages.

Up on the cliff, Reuben paused. He hated heavy seas and heavy rain, especially when they came together, and despite the urgency of Daniel's fate, he stopped to peer down anxiously at the muddy cliff that rose behind his home. There was something not quite right about it.

As he watched, the ladder moved a little, slowly, then slid sideways, to be replaced, as if by magic, with a spouting stream, down which tumbled rocks and clods of earth. Then a stunted tree above the stream sagged and toppled, its roots easing themselves from a pool of grey ooze before following its branches in a lazy slide to the beach below.

Reuben turned to shout his fear at Pin, but Pin had already seen what was happening and followed as Reuben raced towards the beach. They paused on the crumbling cliff where the top of the ladder had been, but the landscape was changing around them as they stood, and below, mud and stony rubble had slid within arm's length of the blind back walls of the cottages.

Reuben plunged forward, sliding and rolling down through the mire. As he leapt too, it occurred to Pin that they might never be able to climb back up.

Molly and Grampy had heard nothing above the noise of the wind, rain and sea, and looked up in alarm as the back door burst open.

'Molly! Grampy! You must get out!' cried Reuben. 'The cliff's falling!'

He dashed back through the door, shouting as he went. 'Pin, help them while I warn Dinah!'

But as Reuben turned to the cottage next door, a great slab of ground above him began to move: the green crust on a giant slice of rock and mud, wider than the cottages themselves, gathering speed as it slithered unstoppably towards him.

10

House Wreck

'Out into the sea!' cried Reuben, as he hurtled through the Olivers' back door. 'Out! Out!'

As he spread his arms at the land crabs, shooing them like a flock of agitated geese, the wall caved in behind him, toppling a dresser lined with crockery, and Dinah screamed, throwing herself towards her children as they ran to the seaward side of the cottage. A boulder crashed through the roof and Reuben felt a heavy gust of air as the attic collapsed into the parlour, and beds and bedding fell around him. Then there were more screams and the roar of water as he was blinded and spun beneath the surf.

When he struggled to his feet, Reuben was outside the cottage. Except there was no cottage. And none next door either. Only the sea, and a small, newly formed promontory of boulders, broken trees and clods of earth, in which pieces of timber roof and wall appeared to have been stuck as random decoration.

'Reuben!'

He staggered round to see Pin, clutching Francis and pulling with his free hand at something in the half-submerged rubble. It was Molly's arm.

'Save your family!' shouted Dinah. 'We can manage.' She'd grabbed the two smallest of her own children from the water and Reuben could see the others, already scrambling out on to what remained of the beach.

Reuben floundered towards Pin and immersed himself beside Molly, pulling at the heaped wet mud and timber that was trapping her legs. To his relief, she kicked free and was soon upright, gasping for breath but with no bones broken. She took Francis, but instead of following Dinah on to the beach, she turned towards what had been her home.

'Where's Grampy?' she cried.

Reuben and Pin struggled after her. They found Grampy's chair, crushed, and then Grampy himself, beneath the flattened, splintered back wall.

'He tried to stop it falling, while we got out the other side,' said Pin, fearing the worst. 'There wasn't time to argue.'

Reuben stared down at the motionless old man, and tears began to well in his eyes.

'Don't look so cheerful,' said a gruff voice. 'I'm not dead.'

*

165

The gaol at Alvershill was small and vile-smelling but the bars on the tiny window were strong and Daniel could see no way of escape.

He looked up as the cell door opened and in came Lieutenant Cade. Daniel was surprised. Somehow, he hadn't expected to come face to face with the officer again.

Lieutenant Cade nodded at him and leant against the wall, careless of the marks left by the mouldering whitewash on his smart blue jacket.

'I have given a full account of events to the magistrate,' he said. 'An indictment is being prepared. That is a formal accusation, Hibberd, to be heard by a court. The magistrate agrees the evidence is sufficient.'

Daniel shook his head in stubborn defiance and Lieutenant Cade shrugged.

'I do not say we would get a verdict here in Alvershill. But in London, before a London jury, composed of London shopkeepers, every man of them sick of the free traders who undercut their prices . . .' He shrugged again. 'You will be consigned to the noose as swiftly as any violent smuggler.'

Lieutenant Cade allowed the naked certainty to sink in, then straightened up.

'Unless there is reason for mercy, of course. In which case your sentence could be commuted to transportation. To the colonies.' He looked at

Daniel. 'Hard labour at first, but there are fortunes to be made by ambitious men who complete their sentence.'

Daniel returned Lieutenant Cade's look steadily.

'And what might the reason be for mercy?'

Lieutenant Cade took a folded packet from his breast pocket and Daniel soon recognized the letter found in his boat. He was already shaking his head as it was opened out before him.

'Tell me who wrote this letter,' urged Lieutenant Cade. 'Or who gave it to you for delivery.'

'I can tell you nothing because I know nothing,' said Daniel wearily.

He laid his head back against the wall. He looked drained and weak, and it occurred to Lieutenant Cade that Daniel might not live to stand trial: gaol fever in London killed more prisoners than the hangman. He slowly refolded the letter and turned to leave.

'Why were you at Chantry Cove?' asked Daniel suddenly. 'Was it because of the London boy?'

Lieutenant Cade paused. There was no harm in telling that much.

'No.'

'He's blamed for the ambush,' said Daniel.

'I cannot help that.'

'My brother too, by some.'

Lieutenant Cade was surprised. 'The Bible bringer?'

Daniel nodded. 'Because he's the London boy's friend. That's why we were on the cliff when you came upon us. I was searching for my brother.'

Lieutenant Cade looked sceptical.

'You do not understand the power of superstition,' said Daniel urgently. 'Reuben saved the London boy from drowning. It's thought such actions bring bad luck. And in some eyes, that's now been more than proved.'

'I don't believe in luck,' replied Lieutenant Cade. 'Only truth and untruth.'

Daniel became passionate.

'Then if you are such an honest man, so fair and upright, why do you not protect the weak? There was no violence in the bay before you came. No damaged nets, no treachery, no murder! You have me locked up safe enough, but it won't end here. The mob will be out. And if Reuben's killed, his blood is on your righteous hands!'

'You fear retribution on your brother?'

'Yes!'

Daniel sat back and swallowed hard, feeling clammy, trying to stay upright.

Lieutenant Cade stared down at him for several seconds. Then turned on his heel and left.

It had been too dangerous to stay on the shore after the landslide because of the likelihood of further cliff falls. And in any case, the rampaging sea had eventually left nothing uncovered, even the high pebble bank at the southern end of the beach, beyond the *Calicut*.

So the Hibberds and the Olivers had retreated, picking their way laboriously up the great chute gouged by the landslide. Their homes, crushed by the elements as easily as any vessel, had no more future now than shipwrecks, and both families salvaged what they could from them before they left.

They had made a shelter on the clifftop out of old torn sailcloth. And though Reuben had fretted about Asher and the rifle as he tied down the makeshift tent, he'd known he couldn't leave. Not yet. With Grampy exhausted and no Daniel, he was needed by his family. And the Olivers, with Bull dead, needed him too, as they struggled to protect themselves from the pelting storm.

But now the storm had spent itself and Reuben had just decided he could fairly leave the bedraggled camp, when a line of fishermen and other villagers appeared, approaching along the cliff with the sunshine. Asher wasn't among them, but Cotton and Noyce were there, and several others who had buried the bad-luck boy.

Reuben was in the tent and didn't see them coming, but Dinah singled out those she knew to be involved and beckoned them forward.

'Come here, my brave boys. Only eight men to

bury a twelve-year-old to his neck? Take a reward for your courage!'

And she hurled the slops of a mackerel bucket at them.

The men recoiled in shock. Only Cotton dared respond.

'How d'you know of that?'

'I know everything.'

''Twas Asher's fault. He made the case. He put us up to it.'

'What are you, sheep?' asked Dinah witheringly. 'Would you walk off a cliff at Asher's command?' She grunted. 'Sheep led by a snake. Don't bleat at me. Explain yourself to the boy himself.'

Reuben appeared. Pin was with him. Dinah was deeply satisfied by the horror-filled reaction of the men, but Reuben hardly noticed. He wanted to be gone.

'No need to stare,' said Dinah. 'He's not risen from the dead. Just rescued. Be sure to tell your Captain Gravedigger.'

'Do the blue-coats know of what we done?' asked Noyce fearfully.

Reuben held his look. 'I'm not a traitor. I told you that before.' He turned dismissively from Noyce and spoke to Dinah and Molly. 'We must go now,' he said. 'The children are safe but Daniel's still in gaol and there's only us to save him.'

And he marched away past the smugglers with his head high, and Pin close on his heels.

Asher lived alone in what had been his mother's house, a damp hovel of tumbledown stone, hidden from the lane by encroaching sycamores and brambles.

Reuben was almost glad to get no answer when knocking at the door: confronting Asher was a dangerous prospect. But they had to find the rifle. The murder weapon.

The door was locked but Pin soon discovered a window at the back, its wooden frame rotted by years of neglect and dripping undergrowth. He patted it once and it disintegrated, the pane smashing noisily on the stone floor within. A pheasant squawked indignantly nearby and the two boys stood motionless, waiting for an angry voice from inside the house. None came, and they clambered through the broken window.

There were just two rooms beyond the scullery in which they first found themselves, and very little furniture besides the litter of bottles and fishing tackle through which they picked their way.

The flagstoned floor of the scullery and parlour changed to wooden boards in the bedroom. Not honey-coloured oak, smelling of beeswax polish as in the display room at Marine View, but dark, musty and rotten, patched here and there with roughly sawn planks, showing the tarry stain of driftwood.

A coat was hanging on the bedroom door. Reuben found nothing in its pockets, and nothing in the rickety cupboard beside the bed. He looked up hopefully as Pin entered from the parlour, but Pin shrugged.

'Nothing in the sideboard,' he said. 'Or the pantry.'

Reuben knelt down and peered under the bed. Nothing there either, except dust and more bottles – but he looked again. There were some newer floorboards beneath the bed, as in other parts of the room, and one of the boards was slightly raised. Reuben reached out and worked his fingers under it, and the whole board moved. It wasn't nailed down. He scrambled to his feet.

'There's a loose board. Let's move the bed.'

Hurriedly, they dragged the bed aside and Reuben lifted the board. The one next to it was also loose and when he'd pulled them both away, Reuben couldn't contain a shout.

'It's here!' he exclaimed. 'The rifle!'

I I

Asher

They lifted out the gun and crouched beside it. There was a box of cartridges as well.

'The blue-coats must believe my brother now!' cried Reuben, laughing with relief. He'd never felt so happy.

'There's no cartridges missing.'

Pin's voice was flat. He'd opened the box.

He looked at Reuben and showed him. The ammunition was tightly packed. To the brim.

Reuben glanced from the box to Pin, as if suspecting some kind of joke. Then he looked quickly again at the rifle. He examined it closely, cocking the hammer, peering down the barrel, sniffing it. When he looked up again, the joyful excitement had gone.

'It's not been fired,' he said, quietly bewildered. He stared at the rifle in his hands, then threw it away so that it clattered across the bare floor. Then he sat staring at the wall in silence for some time, trying to come to terms with the fact that he couldn't, after all, present Lieutenant Cade with both a murder weapon and a murderer.

Pin could think of nothing comforting to say, so he investigated the gap in the floorboards further, lying on his side to peer into the dark narrow space.

'There's something else here, Reuben.'

'What, a dead rat?'

'No . . .' Pin was sitting up again, studying what he'd found. 'It's a bird.'

'What?' Reuben turned, irritated.

Pin was holding an exquisitely small glass dome on a golden plinth. Inside it was an equally exquisite stuffed robin with tiny alert black eyes.

Pin handed his find to Reuben, who frowned.

'Belongs to Mr Pocock,' he said. 'I've seen it at his house.'

Pin had reached under the boards again.

'And there's this,' he said, straightening up and blowing dust from his second discovery. It was a letter. He turned it round in his fingers, peering at the inscription.

'More writing,' he said, giving up.

Reuben took the letter. The seal was unbroken. On the other side was written:

A Septembre
Ile de l'Esperance
Angleterre

'I think it's French,' he said.

Pin was more interested in the robin. It looked valuable on its golden plinth.

'This is worth a pound or two,' he said. 'D'you think he stole it from Mr Pocock?'

'Or was given it,' said Reuben.

'Why would Mr Pocock give Asher a present?' asked Pin, meaning that nobody would.

Reuben didn't answer. Instead, he looked up and said, 'The letter in Daniel's boat was signed by someone called September. And this is *to* September. I saw Asher pass a letter to a Frenchman on the lugger. P'raps he got this one back in exchange and I never noticed.'

Pin was lost. 'So is Asher September?'

Reuben shook his head.

'He can't be. He doesn't read or write.' He looked at the robin, and then at Pin again. 'But Mr Pocock might be. And Asher takes the letters for him.'

Pin stared back, aghast. 'Mr Pocock wants to chop the king's head off?'

Reuben nodded. 'P'raps. And p'raps Asher's with him now.'

They sat in silence for a moment, then put the bed and floorboards back in place, before heading towards Marine View – frightened but determined.

*

As they approached the house, they could hear voices in the clifftop garden – one of them loud, and its angry tone changing and rising in sudden apprehension. It was a rough, thin voice that both boys recognized. It belonged to Asher.

Reuben skirted the high boundary wall that led all the way to the cliff edge, looking for a place to climb. The pillar at the far end was missing, the wall itself stopping raggedly, and Reuben realized there must have been a cliff fall here as well. It wasn't the first time the garden of Marine View had been reduced in such a way: there was no wall at all on the seaward edge of the property, the cliff itself had long since become its boundary. Reuben watched the ground ahead of him cautiously, in case it too was about to slip, and peered round the broken end of the wall.

Asher was in the garden, close to the cliff edge. And so was Mr Pocock. Holding a pistol.

Reuben and Pin shrank back in fright but Asher had seen them and Mr Pocock saw the startled change in Asher's face and spun round. The pistol pointed at Reuben's chest and he froze, terrified.

'Come here, boys,' said Mr Pocock, stepping back so that he could see both them and Asher. He didn't smile and when he spoke again, more sharply, they obeyed, on legs like jelly.

'Come here!'

'Run, boys, run!' urged Asher, as they approached.

'He's a murderer. 'Twas him shot Boatman Gibbs. I saw him. I was there!'

'Ignore him, he's a wicked man,' said Mr Pocock shortly. 'He thinks if you run, I'll shoot at you and have no lead ball left for him.'

'He shot Gibbs with that very pistol!' cried Asher. 'We had a meetin' on the cliff and Gibbs blundered in on us. 'Twas cold blood. Run, damn you!'

But Reuben was afraid to run and so was Pin. And Reuben stared at Mr Pocock, trembling.

'Did you, sir? Was it you shot Boatman Gibbs?'

'It was,' said Mr Pocock curtly. 'Why? Are you sorry for the death of such a brute?'

'Aye, sir,' cried Reuben, fighting hot tears, 'when my brother's to hang for a murder done by you!'

Mr Pocock kept careful watch on all of them as he replied. His voice was steady, unrepentant.

'Don't think that I'm afraid to face the law myself,' he said. 'But I'm more useful still alive than dead. The Cause itself is more important than one man, even your brother.'

Reuben, reckless in his misery, made to speak but Mr Pocock stopped him.

'Listen to me, Reuben,' he demanded. 'And you, boy.' He glanced fiercely at Pin, though the fierceness seemed to Pin not cruel but strangely beseeching.

'The Cause is just,' insisted Mr Pocock. He

looked again at Reuben. 'Your brother is a brave and honest man. He would approve.'

'No!'

'Yes! Hear me out. You are poor: you have nothing. And it is poverty that keeps the people of this country in chains, Reuben. And the people of France, despite their brief and glorious revolution. The people of Italy and Spain, the people of all Europe suffer. For poverty suits the ruling class of every nation. Rich men build factories and grow richer still by paying a pittance to those whose backs they break. Rich farmers drive families from their land to make more room to hunt a fox for pleasure. Can that be right? Why, the seabirds on the Cormorant Cliff have more freedom than the poor! But if every man was equal; if there were no kings, no aristocracy; if instead there was a parliament where every man of every class had equal say, would that not change things for the better? That is our Cause. That is what we long and fight for, Reuben. You are brave and honest too, and young. Join me, both of you. Help change this world. Were there kings and lords in the Garden of Eden?'

'But my brother, sir!' cried Reuben.

And Asher, who had sneered and scoffed throughout the speech, while he gauged the risk of running, thought Reuben might now be rash enough to act.

'Aye, tell him, Reuben,' he exhorted. 'Tell the murdering dog. Take him down, the pair of you!'

'Don't dare to speak to these young men!' Mr Pocock turned on Asher with fierce contempt. 'You that will do nothing ever except for money. And when gold's been stuffed in your outstretched grubby hand, still demand more. Always more. Give me the letter now,' he insisted. 'And for nothing. Not the double price you came here wanting. The letter. Now!'

He cocked the pistol, and Asher knew he would use it.

'I haven't brought it, sir.' His tone became instantly humble. 'I told you so. It's true. You may search me, if you wish.'

'True?' Mr Pocock spat the word. 'What is there about you that is true? Where is the letter!'

'In my house, sir. Safely hidden, where I always keep them. I'm very careful, sir. Beneath the boards.'

And Mr Pocock caught the fatal glance that passed between Pin and Reuben.

Questions suddenly occurred to him. 'Why did you come here?' he asked abruptly.

Reuben was too slow in answering.

'What do you know of the letter? Have you found it?'

Neither boy spoke.

'Turn out your pockets,' ordered Mr Pocock. Reuben looked at Pin then slowly produced the unopened letter. Mr Pocock snatched it.

'Well, well.' He tucked the letter securely inside his jacket and smiled. 'We'll make agents of you yet.' Then he looked at Asher.

'You may leave us,' he said.

Asher hesitated, confused, looking from Mr Pocock to the boys and back again, then took a step towards the broken end of the wall.

'No, no,' said Mr Pocock calmly. 'That way.' And he waved the pistol at the sea, then pointed it at Asher and advanced towards him.

'No . . .' moaned Asher. 'No . . . You can't do this . . .'

'Why waste a pistol ball?' asked Mr Pocock. 'Unless you insist.'

'Help me, lads, for pity's sake!' screamed Asher, but as the words left him so did his foothold on the cliff edge and he disappeared in a scrabble of flailing hands and crumbling chalk.

Reuben forgot the pistol and ran to the cliff edge. He could hear a kind of broken whimper and, looking down, saw Asher, still alive.

He'd fetched up on a pile of fallen chalk, halfway between the clifftop and the boiling sea below, and lay clinging pitifully to a tree root embedded in the shifting chalk. Each time he moved, the chalk and tree root slipped a little further.

On seeing Reuben up above, Asher, though in pain, became agitated.

'Throw me a rope, Reuben,' he gabbled eagerly. 'Save me and I'll save your brother. I'll testify. I promise! And I'm sorry for what happened at Black Tooth. Forgive me, lad, forgive me. Let's help each other, eh? Speak, damn you, boy! Throw a rope!' His expression changed, as if suddenly he'd found the answer. 'Is it money that you want?'

He took one hand from the tree root and feverishly pulled a leather bag from his pocket, balancing precariously as he shook it in the air.

'Here, Reuben, here. I've got money, see? Fifty pounds. Save me and it's yours, every last penny! Fifty pounds, Reuben! I don't want it, I don't want it. Do me a double kindness, take it from me. Blood money, boy. From the blue-coats. 'Twas me who laid the information. Pocock's right, I was mad for money. But I'm confessing, hear me? I'm a changed man. I repent. I'm sorry for Black Tooth. I'm sorry for Chantry Cove. Save me, Reuben! Save me, damn you!'

A hand on Reuben's rigid shoulder made him start.

'Come away,' said Mr Pocock. 'You've heard what he has to say. He's no more loss to us than Boatman Gibbs.'

Reuben resisted but Mr Pocock was stronger

and pulled him up, pointing the pistol now at Pin, to bring him close.

'So then, boys.' Mr Pocock's voice was low, excited. 'Join me, both of you, keep my secret, and Daniel *will* be saved. I'll swear to any court that it was Asher who killed Gibbs. That I came upon him rolling drunk and in that state he boasted of the deed, a pistol shot. Whereupon I tried to apprehend him and he fell and drowned. And took the pistol with him. My word is good. And Lieutenant Cade is thorough: Asher's body will be found without a wound. Gibbs's body will be examined and the pistol ball be found in him. Not a rifle bullet. But the pistol will be gone forever. I'll throw it in the sea, right now. Your brother will go free.'

Reuben was already shaking his head.

'But it's a lie! *You* murdered Boatman Gibbs!'

'Trust me, Reuben, as I'm trusting you!'

To seal the bargain he was certain would be honoured, Mr Pocock strode to the cliff edge, stood a moment, then hurled the pistol high and far. And Asher, seeing the man and gun above him, thought he was to be shot after all and flinched away, and started falling.

Reuben heard the great howl of despair and the sliding rumble, and could only watch while Asher was carried into the sea, still vainly clutching the tree root. The mass of dirty chalk hissed and sank in the water, turning it the colour of porridge, and Asher reappeared briefly before a wave dashed him against the rocks.

Reuben gazed down and temptation whispered in his ear. Let Asher die: doesn't he deserve it? Let Mr Pocock tell the lie: free Daniel. Free Daniel. It was so easy. He need do nothing. Literally nothing.

And Reuben hated Asher. That was his last bewildering thought as he dodged away from Mr Pocock and slid and tumbled down the cliff to try to save the drowning man.

Justice

Mr Pocock stared in shock but quickly reassured himself: he had the letter. That was the all-important thing. Safe in his pocket to be read later. News from January of when help would come. News of plots, of assassinations. Of Bold and Ardent Hopes fulfilled. But he must keep the London boy close till Reuben's fate was clear. He didn't doubt that Asher would drown: he knew he couldn't swim.

Mr Pocock regretted the gesture with the pistol and clutched Pin's arm instead, pulling him towards the open French windows of the house. Pin dug in his heels and tried to bite and punch, but he was even less of a match for Mr Pocock than Reuben had been and was soon dragged across the threshold into the display room.

There, though, he wedged himself doggedly against a heavy table lined with domes and cases, and Mr Pocock briefly lost his footing on the polished floor. He grabbed the table as he fell, but as he hauled his weight up on the other side, Pin pushed with all his might and set the table falling. It crashed across Mr Pocock, who heard an explosion of glass, before he saw birds settling around him and the darting beak of a cormorant right before his closing eyes.

Pin surveyed the overturned table and shattered display cases with some pride. He was stronger than he'd thought. The table wasn't heavy enough to have crushed Mr Pocock, but he lay motionless, having cracked his head. Pin leant gingerly across the splintered glass to make sure the man was still breathing, then ran from door to door, turning and removing keys, before dashing out to find his friend.

It was not like saving Pin had been. Not standing on firm land and pulling. Reuben couldn't swim but he would have to now. Asher had disappeared twice and each time he re-emerged there was less life in his eyes. Each rebounding wave carried him further from the rocks where Reuben stood and wavered. Jump now or not at all. Reuben jumped.

The sea closed over him as it had briefly at Black Tooth and in the flattened cottage. But now there was nothing beneath his feet. Just more water. Deep. Deep.

Reuben kicked his feet and surfaced, disorientated, looking wildly around for Asher, then saw him in the trough of a wave. He seemed further away than ever. Reuben kicked again and went on kicking, reaching out with his hands and dragging at the sea, clawing his way forward, telling himself again and again that it was just like climbing across a flat wet cliff.

He stretched out and seized Asher's hair, the only part of him that he could see, then got a hand beneath his arm and lifted. Nothing happened except that they both sank and Reuben knew he too was finally going to drown. He came up again, gagging on salt water but still holding Asher, and found by accident that by leaning back instead of forward he could support him better and make some progress by kicking like a frog.

Gradually the cliff drew closer, but as it did, Asher began to stir, coughing, and moving his arms so that Reuben almost lost him. And there was still the huge difficulty of getting back ashore. Reuben tried to kick towards the easiest-looking spot but the waves surged round and over him and swept him against a sheer rock face, impossible to grab.

Asher was finally slipping from his grasp when something slapped the sea beside them: a lobster pot, broken and barnacled, dredged up by the storm, together with its frayed and knotted line. The line rose vertically into the air, and at its other end, clinging to the slippery rock above, was Pin.

Reuben grabbed the pot and clung on one-handed as he and Asher were banged and scraped along the rock face, hauled in like heavy inedible fish. Step by step, Pin dragged them through the waves to a lower place, where he could land them. But when at last he lashed the ancient line round a slender point of rock, the fibres snapped and though he grasped Reuben's hand in time, the combined weight of two bodies soon had him slithering inexorably towards the drop.

'Hold him, London boy!'

The shout from behind Pin was more an order than encouragement. Hands grabbed his legs, and others reached down past him, taking hold of Reuben and then Asher. Strong arms. With blue sleeves.

Mr Pocock stirred, sat up. Cut his hand on broken glass. Remembered where he was and why, and clambered hastily to his feet, despite the throbbing of his head. The London boy had gone. And what of Reuben? He hurried to the French windows, which were shut. Turned the handles and found them locked. A figure loomed outside. Mr Pocock recognized the chief officer of coastguards. Astonishingly, he held a key that Mr Pocock also recognized. He put it in the lock and turned it.

'Good day, sir,' said the officer politely, as he let in fresh sea air. 'We have a man outside called

Asher. Grateful to be alive. A most talkative fellow, as we have found before. Do you know him?'

'A rogue. He's nothing to me.' Mr Pocock tried not to bluster.

Lieutenant Cade made no comment. He looked gravely at Mr Pocock.

'Would you have a letter in your pocket, sir? From January?'

A crowd had gathered by Marine View, drawn initially by the cliff fall, which they'd seen from along the bay.

They watched and whispered as first Asher, then nice Mr Pocock, and then a box of books and papers were carried off. And wondered what was being said as the coastguard officer shook the hand of Reuben Hibberd.

'And my brother, sir?' asked Reuben, still anxious despite the thanks and praise that he'd been given.

'Is free, of course. With my apology.' Lieutenant Cade paused. He looked towards the house and frowned, seeing a man walking towards them, escorted by a blue-coat.

Without a word, he pulled Reuben away beyond the broken wall and, to the boy's astonishment, scooped a handful of mud from the sodden cliff edge and smeared it liberally on Reuben's face.

'He's come in hope of a reward,' murmured Lieutenant Cade. 'To identify a suspect. Stand still.'

Through caked eyelids, Reuben recognized the man from Alvershill to whom he'd tried to sell the rifle. The man stopped, disconcerted.

'Well?' demanded Lieutenant Cade. 'Is this the boy?'

'How can I tell?' complained the man. 'Can't you wash his face?'

'He lives on the shore,' replied Lieutenant Cade. 'They're always dirty. Can you identify him or not? Quickly.'

The man peered but dared not scrape away the mud.

'No,' he admitted.

'Then the boy goes free and you've had a wasted journey. Good day to you.'

The man was reluctant to leave but Lieutenant Cade looked sharply at the blue-coat, who obediently led him away, with a confused backward glance of his own.

Lieutenant Cade smiled.

'Good luck, Reuben. But don't forget: I remain the enemy of smugglers.' He paused. 'Oh, and I'd be obliged if the case of rifles missing from the wreck was to appear outside the coastguard station when my back is turned. Which it will be, at midnight.'

He nodded a farewell, mounted his great black horse and rode away.

It was a squash.

Thirteen people round one table, even if one of them was a baby on a lap. A strange table too: an upturned boat with planks across it. But the food was good. Dinah had decreed a non-mackerel day. So there was bread and cheese, and more bread. And beer. And two chickens from Farmer Toogood. And a cake from Parson Teague, which surprised everyone, Hibberds and Olivers.

Grampy tried it first, dubiously, and chewed a long time.

'Like his sermons,' he pronounced. 'Dry and hard to swallow.'

Everyone laughed but was grateful, nonetheless. It was a day for gratitude and cheerfulness, even if you didn't have a house to live in. The sun was shining.

'So are you staying with us, Pin?' asked Molly suddenly. 'Or will you take another ship to India?'

The question took him by surprise. Pin had quite forgotten banquets under palm trees and the beguiling lack of frostbite. He looked around the expectant smiling faces. Instead of no family, he now had two. And he had the rest of his life to ride an elephant. He shrugged.

'Well, I suppose I'd better stay,' he said. 'To go

bird huntin' on the cliffs. Reuben's such a lump –
it's him that caused the landslides.'

And everyone laughed, even Reuben.

'Aye,' said Daniel, 'you must come in the boat
with me now, brother, and sink that instead.'

'He will sink it. No doubt of that,' growled
Grampy. 'He's snatched two lives from the sea now,
not just one. That's double bad luck.'

Dinah glared at him. 'You old fool,' she said
indignantly. 'You're talking fish guts.'

Then she caught his eye and realized he was
joking and threw a hunk of bread at him.

Fred Mew's excellent book of memories, *Back of the Wight*, provided the inspiration for the mackerel-catching episode in this novel.

Beliefs concerning bargains with the sea and ownership of what is washed up by it have a long history but are cogently described in Bella Bathurst's book *The Wreckers*.

BLOOD-SOAKED BATTLES
and evil plots . . .

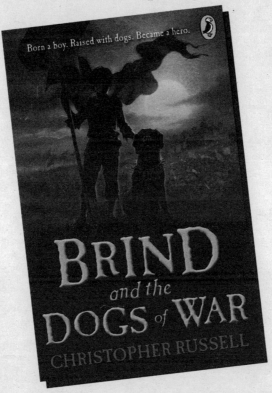

Brind, the dog boy, is thrown into a world more dangerous than the fiercest of his dogs – the world of men.

SHORTLISTED FOR THE GUARDIAN CHILDREN'S FICTION PRIZE

puffin.co.uk

THE BLACK DEATH
The most terrible of plagues is
sweeping across England.

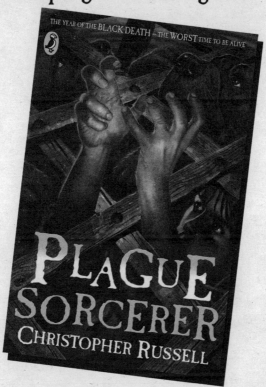

People are looking for someone to blame,
someone like Brind, the dog boy.

*They say he's a witch — and suddenly
Brind has to run for his life.*

puffin.co.uk

Choosing a brilliant book
can be a tricky business...
but not any more

www.puffin.co.uk

The best selection of books at your fingertips

So get clicking!

Searching the site is easy – you'll find
what you're looking for at the click of a mouse,
from great authors to brilliant books and more!

Puffin by Post

Smugglers – Christopher Russell

If you have enjoyed this book and want to read more,
then check out these other great Puffin titles.
You can order any of the following books direct with Puffin by Post:

Brind and the Dogs • Christopher Russell • 0141318546	£4.99
'Original and hugely satisfying' – *Guardian*	

Plague Sorcerer • Christopher Russell • 0141318554	£4.99
'Admirably vivid . . . cliff-hanging action' – *Books for Keeps*	

Barkbelly • Cat Weatherill • 0141381167	£9.99
'A magical book' – Michael Morpurgo	

The Whispering Road • Livi Michael • 0141317035	£5.99
'A powerful and quite extraordinary novel' – Berlie Doherty	

Time Bomb • Nigel Hinton • 0141318333	£4.99
'It hooked me completely. I loved it' – Michelle Magorian	

Just contact:

Puffin Books, c/o Bookpost, PO Box 29,
Douglas, Isle of Man, IM99 1BQ
Credit cards accepted. For further details:
Telephone: 01624 677237
Fax: 01624 670923

You can email your orders to: bookshop@enterprise.net
Or order online at: www.bookpost.co.uk

Free delivery in the UK.
Overseas customers must add £2 per book.

Prices and availability are subject to change.

Visit puffin.co.uk to find out about the latest titles, read extracts and
exclusive author interviews, and enter exciting competitions.
You can also browse thousands of Puffin books online.